COME BACK TO ME

God, she wished he hadn't done that—gotten close to her. The scent of masculine cologne drifted over and she could barely breathe. Her heart beat erratically as Zan's thigh pressed against her leg. She assumed that had happened accidentally. But when he looked at her, she forgot why she was here. Better to concentrate on the sandwich that now lodged in her throat and not on the man who'd made it difficult to digest.

Come
BACK TO ME

Marcia King-Gamble

ARABESQUE

BET BOOKS

BET Publications, LLC
http://www.bet.com
http://www.arabesquebooks.com

ARABESQUE BOOKS are published by

BET Publications, LLC
c/o BET BOOKS
One BET Plaza
1900 W Place NE
Washington, DC 20018-1211

All Kensington Titles, Imprints, and Distributed Lines are available at special quantity discounts for bulk purchases for sales promotions, premiums, fund-raising, and educational or institutional use. Special book excerpts or customized printings can also be created to fit specific needs. For details, write or phone the office of the Kensington special sales manager: Kensington Publishing Corp., 850 Third Avenue, New York, NY 10022, attn: Special Sales Department, Phone: 1-800-221-2647.

First Printing: February 2004
10 9 8 7 6 5 4 3 2 1

Printed in the United States of America

For all the missing children, and for the parents whose lives are now a living hell. May you soon be reunited. To my dear friend, Liz Etkind. Why? Because you've always been there for me, and because you asked.

Chapter 1

The woman's dainty hands were the first things Zan McManus noted. They were folded in her lap, birdlike and fragile. It made him wonder if when he shook one it would break.

"Mrs. Phillips?" Zan inquired, looking into a stunning face, heart-shaped and vulnerable, huge golden eyes brimming with tears.

"Ms. Phillips," she corrected, in a husky voice that indicated she was close to the breaking point. "I'm no longer married and I've taken my maiden name back. You may call me Kristie if you prefer."

The name suited her. She looked like a black porcelain doll that required care.

"Okay, Kristie," Zan said. "Please follow me."

At that point he offered her his hand. Kristie shook it and as he expected, it felt like parchment. He could tell that she was nervous and on the edge.

Zan could feel his legal assistant Miriam's eyes on his back as the woman stood. She came up to his chest. Her slender frame boasted legs made longer by three-inch heels. She had golden skin and wore her vulnerability on her sleeve. He stood aside, ushering her into his office, while Miriam gaped. Normally that was her job.

"I'll shut the door," Miriam said, rising and yanking on the brass knob after they'd entered.

"Water?" Zan offered, striding toward the cooler he kept for that very purpose. Most of his clients were nervous their first time around.

Zan's spacious corner office overlooked Hempstead Avenue, a busy intersection on Long Island, New York.

Kristie pulled herself together, nodding her assent. "Yes, I would love some water, please."

Zan filled a paper cup and handed it to the woman, who remained standing. She sipped on it slowly.

He remembered his manners, gesturing to one of the comfortable burgundy wingback chairs with brass studs running the perimeters. "Please take a seat."

Kristie Phillips sat, crossing one slender leg over the other. Beautiful legs, he might add. Zan had always been a leg man and knew a dynamite pair when he saw them. Kristie Phillips's blew you away. He cleared his throat, using that time to regroup. Ms. Phillips was the client. He must remember that.

Miriam had filled him in. The woman desperately needed his help. Her six-year-old son had disappeared and her ex-husband was the culprit. Like most other women in her predicament she had very little money, but would sell her soul if it meant getting her child back.

Zan had a soft spot for cases like these. He practiced family law and nothing surprised him anymore. It was a wonder he wasn't jaded. Kristie Phillips had been referred by a friend of a client. Someone whom he'd helped when her Iranian husband left, supposedly for a vacation, taking her son with him. It had taken years, but eventually they had been successful in getting the boy out of Tehran. He now resided with his mother in the United States.

"Why don't you start your story from the beginning, Ms. Phillips?" Zan said, taking a seat behind the huge mahogany desk he had inherited from his adoptive grandfather who'd also been an attorney.

"I'm not sure where to start," she said, twisting her hands this way and that, trying to keep her voice steady.

"Tell me how your ex happened to get possession of your son."

A heart-shaped face, golden eyes pooling, stared back at him. Zan, stood, slid a desk drawer open, and silently handed her some Kleenex. He strode to the window and pretended to stare out at the traffic, giving her time to compose herself.

"I'm so sorry," Kristie said, catching herself. "I'm not usually like this, but I miss my son and I swear I could kill that no-good son of——" A tiny fist pounded the desk and she managed a brave smile.

"It's all right. I guess l would feel the same way."

There was steel beneath that fragile exterior. Good. Kristie Phillips would need all the steel she could muster by the time they were through.

"What's your son's name?" Zan asked, resuming his seat and reaching for the Mont Blanc pen on his desk to scribble on an open pad.

"Curtis."

"That's a fine name for a young man," Zan said, writing it down. "And his father's?"

Kristie looked like she would be sick. She spat the name out. "Earl Leone."

Zan wrote that down as well. He wondered what kind of man Earl was who would give up a wife that looked like this. "How did Earl get possession of Curtis?"

Kristie looked like she wanted to throw up, one hand clutching her chest. "He picked him up as usual on a Friday as our agreement stipulated. Regrettably he has weekend visitation rights."

"And he never returned him, I take it." One of Zan's eyebrows rose, though he had heard the story before, more often than he cared to recount.

"No, I haven't seen my baby since."

Kristie's eyes brimmed with tears. One of them spilled onto her cheekbone. He wanted to reach over and use his own fingers to wipe the moisture away but knew it would not be proper. He wanted to take her frail body into his arms, nestle her straightened cap of streaked brown curls under his chin, and comfort her. He had the feeling Kristie Phillips needed a good hug, and had needed one for quite some time. But she was his client, and professionalism alone mandated he keep his distance.

Zan's voice was gruffer than he intended it to be. "Okay, now, I know this is going to be difficult, but I want you to think about the day Curtis disappeared. Tell me when you last saw or spoke to him or his father. No detail is unimportant. The more I have the more I may be able to help you. We may eventually have to resort to hiring a detective, but right now let's see what we can piece together."

"A private detective?" Kristie cried, jumping to her feet. "I don't have the money for a private detective. I don't even know how I'm going to manage your fee."

"Ms. Phillips, please calm down. We'll work out the financial details later."

This time Zan did leave the safety of his desk and cross over to her. He placed a stilling hand on her shoulder. "Right now our only mission is to find your little boy and get him home safely."

Again, Zan resisted the urge to wrap his arms around Kristie's compact body and absorb the pain that seemed to flow through every pore. She stared up at him with those moist amber eyes, her full bottom lip quivering. God, she must be a heartbreaker when all fixed up. Even now with mascara rimming her eyes, and what looked to be a hastily pulled on skirt and blouse, she gave Halle Berry a run for her money. No easy task.

"Do you really think you can find my boy?" Kristie asked, shoulders heaving.

"I'll try my best."

"Then I'll find the money somewhere."

Zan didn't believe in making false promises. He owed it to his clients to be truthful, and he'd pretty much made up his mind that Kristie Phillips would be a client, pro bono or otherwise.

He gave her arm another reassuring pat, realizing she was skin and bones.

Zan intended to help because his instincts were to protect, and because he'd been one of those missing children. It had taken him almost twenty-

one years to find his mother. And when he did, it
had been too late.

Kristie Phillips stared down at the cuff of a crisp
monogrammed white shirt, a sharp contrast from
the attorney's pecan-colored hand. He had long
slender fingers with clipped nails. Those fingers patted her arm rhythmically. T. Zan McManus had been
recommended by a friend of a friend, and though
she'd heard he commanded a huge fee, a fee she
could never possibly afford, in desperation she had
come to him.

The posh waiting area with its leather furniture
and lined bookshelves shouted affluence. Still she'd
enjoyed looking at the paintings and huge potted
plants; they'd added humanity to the room. Kristie
had been too absorbed by her predicament to give
T. Zan McManus more than a cursory glance when
he'd greeted her warmly and ushered her into his
office. But now she took a deep breath and stepped
back.

Zan's touch had unsettled her. He caught himself
and returned to sit behind that huge desk, fumbling
to find the horn-rimmed glasses slightly out of his
reach. All business, he shoved them onto his face.

"Well, now," T. Zan said, clearing his throat.
"Please think back to the day when you discovered
Curtis was missing. Tell me what you are able to re-
call when you are ready."

How to begin? How to make this man understand that she'd done everything in her power to
keep her marriage together? A marriage whose foun-
dation had never been built on love but rather de-

pendency. Of course she hadn't realized that when she'd first met Earl, she'd been too young. And even after the divorce when it was clear that he wasn't the role model that her son needed, she'd made sure that father and son saw each other on weekends as the judge had mandated. She owed it to her boy.

"It was last Sunday night," Kristie began, her voice going shaky again. "Normally Earl picks Curtis up from school on Friday and he returns him on Sunday after dinner."

She could feel the anger build, frustration constricting her vocal cords. Her head pounded and her chest felt as if it had been run over by a steamroller. It had been that way since the day she'd been forced to face the awful truth. Earl had run off with her baby.

T. Zan McManus handed Kristie another fistful of tissues. What a fool she was making of herself in front of him. She accepted the tissues and with moist eyes nodded her thanks. He stared back at her. The voltage from those gray eyes threatened to short-circuit her already shallow breathing. But she held his glance, staring back, mesmerized by the intensity of his gaze.

The man's shoulders were the size of a football player's, stretching his crisp white shirt to the max. A corded neck peeking over the top of his buttoned-down collar indicated the unleashed strength he possessed. His head was shaved and his face model-hard as if chiseled from stone. Those gray compassionate eyes held hers, daring her to look away. But it was his mouth that drew her and those lips that tilted up slightly at the corners. When he spoke, the cleft in his chin deepened. Something about his whole appearance told her she could trust him.

It was the first time in a long time Kristie had had such a strong reaction to a man. She didn't know what to make of it, nor did she have the time or inclination to consider what it might mean. She was here in his office for one reason. She needed his help.

"No, Earl didn't bring Curtis home, and I began to worry when he didn't call. So I phoned him, got his answering machine, and left a message. I became frantic later that evening. At first I thought he might have been in a car accident and I started calling hospitals, with no luck. Then I phoned the police, but they wouldn't take a missing person's report, because less than twenty-four hours had elapsed."

"So what did you do?" T. Zan asked in the kindest of tones. "By the way, the twenty-four-hour rule doesn't apply to a missing child."

She'd been given the wrong information. She could kill the stupid operator who'd cost her valuable time.

"I got into my car," she said, "even though I knew it was stupid to go alone to Earl's that late at night. But I wanted my child and desperation makes you do stupid things. It was foolish of me."

"Why foolish?"

Kristie hesitated, reluctant to unload on a stranger.

T. Zan removed his glasses and set them down on the huge desk separating them. His eyes never left her face.

"Were you afraid of Earl?" he asked softly.

"Petrified. I had reason to be."

"Did he threaten you?"

It was worse than that. What would he say if she told him about the beatings? But it seemed sacrilegious to air her dirty laundry to a man she'd just met, albeit an attorney. She wasn't here for that.

"He . . . uh . . . he . . . Let's just say Earl had his problems. "

T. Zan stood, splaying large hands on the desk. "What kind of problems?"

"Substance dependence."

The grim expression on T. Zan's face frightened her. She could tell by the way his jaw muscles worked that he would be a force to be reckoned with if he ever got angry, truly angry. And he was furious. Why?

"Earl had a bad temper," Kristie admitted, lowering her eyes.

"Did he hit you?"

Hit would be putting it mildly. Earl's fists had pounded her relentlessly. When she made him angry he would hurl things, even her furniture. She could still hear the heartbreaking voice of her child pleading with his father to stop hurting Mommy. That was what had given her the courage to leave him. She didn't want Curtis growing up thinking that it was acceptable for a man to hit a woman.

T. Zan waited for an answer but no words would come.

"Well, did he?" the attorney pressed.

The room was suddenly warm, the spring breeze coming through the window doing nothing to ease her heat or discomfort. Even now she could still smell Earl's liquored-up breath as his clenched fists drove into her stomach. Her hands often rose to

her face, protecting the only thing that she had
left: a presentable face, one that once helped her
earn money as a print model.

"He did," she admitted, hoping that he would
not judge her or think that she was one of those
women who truly believed that her husband beat
her because he loved her.

"Bastard," T. Zan spat out, leaving the safety of
the barricade that separated them and stalking the
perimeters of the room. He pulled up another wingback chair and took a seat beside her. An expensive-
looking loafer swung back and forth.

"Tell me," he urged. "You drove alone to Earl's
place and what did you find when you got there?"

"The house was in darkness. I immediately knew
something was wrong."

She couldn't continue. Couldn't admit that re-
living the nightmare was taking a toll on her. Had
taken a toll on her. She was close to losing her sanity, and each day that passed made her miss Curtis
more. Hopelessness now engulfed her and she
resided in a dark place nursing her pain.

Warm fingers massaged the nape of her neck as
T. Zan urged her to take deep breaths, to breathe
in and out slowly.

Kristie did, enjoying the soothing hands against
her flesh and T. Zan's quiet but authoritative voice,
telling her that she would be okay. He would rep-
resent her and would do his best to get Curtis back
to her safely.

Curtis's name reminded her she needed to be
strong. She refused the wad of tissues T. Zan was
about to hand to her and sniffed loudly.

"That's enough for today," her newly hired attorney said, reaching for the pad on his desk and the expensive Mont Blanc pen that cost more than her monthly electric bill. "Write your address and phone number down. Will you be okay to drive?"

Kristie managed to nod. But she didn't feel okay to drive. She hadn't felt okay to do a thing in the last couple of days. Not since Earl had abducted her child, ripping her heart out in the process.

T. Zan surprised Kristie by walking her out. His assistant seemed equally as astounded as he strode past, keeping a firm hold on Kristie's elbow.

Outside on Hempstead Avenue, traffic zoomed by and a breeze ruffled the buds of blooming trees. Spring was definitely in the air in this New York suburban town, but spring was not in Kristie's heart as she hurried toward her aging Toyota parked on a side street, her attorney beside her.

She stopped in front of her beat-up car, fumbled in her purse, and extracted her keys. T. Zan stuck out his hand.

"We'll talk soon," he said.

Kristie shook his hand, wondering where she would find the money to pay a high-priced attorney of his stature.

"You have my card?" T. Zan asked.

Kristie nodded. She'd tucked his card in one of the compartments of her purse the moment Lizette Stokes, her best friend and coworker at the school where they taught special-needs kids, had given it to her.

T. Zan held out his open palm and motioned with his chin that he expected her to turn over her car keys. The man couldn't possibly be thinking of driving her home. Yet there was something about him that she trusted and she silently gave up her keys.

He unlocked the car and stood aside while she slid into the driver's seat. When he leaned over and stuck the keys in the ignition, she got a whiff of a manly scent that made her a little bit dizzy. He stood back, waving her off.

It took Kristie a full ten minutes to get it together. It wasn't until she was on Southern State heading for the Baldwin exit and her home that she fully recovered. She didn't know what she had expected when Lizette had suggested she see an attorney, but it wasn't this, a man that looked as if he had stepped off the cover of *GQ* and was both charming and formidable.

The little Cape Cod house that she'd inherited seemed empty and lifeless now that Curtis was gone. His bike remained in the same hastily abandoned angle where he'd left it. She knew she risked theft but hadn't had the heart to put it away.

Inside, the house was dark and spotless. A red light blinked on the answering machine. Holding her breath, Kristie depressed the button, hoping against all odds that Earl had left her a message, telling her that her rambunctious son was too much for him to handle and she should come and get him.

No such luck. Lizette's high-pitched voice filled Kristie's ear.

"So?" her friend inquired. "Is Zan McManus able to help you? Call me the minute you get in."

Kristie needed to talk to someone. At times like this, when she was alone in the house she doubted her sanity. Work structured her life and was the only thing she could count on. It gave her purpose. She had taken the day off to see to this business, and the rest of the afternoon and evening loomed ahead. When darkness fell, fears and doubts would crowd it. She didn't trust Earl with her child. His boozing and pill popping had rendered him an irresponsible parent. A child of Curtis's age needed a firm hand and constant supervision. Earl was incapable of providing the guidance Curtis needed.

Kristie picked up her son's photograph from the top of the piano and stared into her little boy's face.

"Please be all right," she whispered.

Curtis was the spitting image of the man she once needed. He had a cherub's face with golden skin and a smile a mile wide. She had given him five bucks only a few weeks ago for that missing tooth. Kristie sat on the four-poster bed, found the cordless phone, and punched the buttons. Lizette answered on the fourth ring.

"How did it go?"

Caller ID made identifying oneself unnecessary.

"Okay, I guess."

"Just okay?"

"I liked Mr. McManus."

"Good." There was a pause and then Lizette said, "From everything I've heard he's drop-dead gorgeous."

Kristie refused to comment. It was T. Zan's legal expertise that she needed, not his looks.

"That's irrelevant to me," she said. "I need an attorney with a killer instinct, not a supermodel face."

"He came with high recommendations. Paula told me she used him to get her son back. It was tough getting him out of Tehran but somehow T. Zan did it, enlisting Interpol and the State Department's help."

"My situation is different," Kristie reminded her. "I'm a lowly peon who doesn't have the money to pay the attorney's fee."

"McManus helped another woman whose ex forged a note and came to his son's school to pick him up," Lizette said patiently. "The father took the child out of state but Zan got him back. How's that case different from yours?"

Good point. Kristie had heard the story over and over. The woman's son had managed to call his mother on his own. He'd barely gotten out that he was at Grandma's before his father had caught on. T. Zan McManus had contacted the cops. Within twenty-four hours mother and son had been re-united. But how much had that cost?

It had been two days, fifteen hours, thirty-four minutes since her child had been gone and she'd ceased breathing.

"Kristie, are you there?" Lizette's anxious voice penetrated the fog.

"I'm here," Kristie said more calmly than she felt.

"Let me take you out for drinks and dinner on the water."

She realized she hadn't eaten all day. Food sounded good and drinks might help her forget. Besides, she needed a sounding board and Lizette was a good listener.

"I shouldn't leave the house. What if Curtis calls?"

"Forward your calls to your cell phone and tell your neighbors that you're going out. I'll be there within the hour," said Lizette, who lived fairly close by in Malverne.

A tone resounded in Kristie's ear. Call waiting had kicked in. She ended the conversation and quickly pushed a button. T. Zan McManus's gritty voice filled her ear.

"Just checking on you, Kristie, making sure that you got home safely."

"I did, and thanks."

Kristie's hand clutched the receiver. Zan's phone inquiry was way beyond the call of duty. She didn't quite know what to make of it. A warm feeling suffused her; must be stress.

Somehow, some way, she would find the money to pay T. Zan McManus.

If it meant prostituting herself she would get her child back.

Chapter 2

Zan McManus was at the gym in the middle of abdominal crunches when an image of Kristie Phillips surfaced. Her face kept popping up at the most unexpected times and he meant to call her when he got back to his office. But right now he needed to complete his workout; it was necessary to keep his stress level down.

A redheaded woman strutted by and not for the first time. Her cosmetically enhanced breasts overflowed a skimpy black top, and excessive gold jewelry jangled as she bounced. She eyed him, smiled, and began stretching out on a mat alongside him.

Definitely not his type. He liked his women classy and far less obvious. Besides, he had no time for casual dalliances. His work was draining enough.

"Hey, do you come here often?" The redhead huffed, turning slightly and grabbing her leg. Her nipples strained against the thin black material of the midriff top.

"Not as often as I would like," Zan answered, continuing his crunches.

She smiled at him. Her face was not unattractive. But the predatory look in her eye, one that he was familiar with, turned him off.

"When exactly do you come?" she asked.

Zan wished she would button it up or simply remove herself to another location. He suspected she was one of those rich, spoiled women from nearby Garden City with too much time on her hands.

"Whenever I get the chance," he answered evasively.

"And just when is that?"

He took his time answering, hoping she would get the message. Maybe it was time to go to the weight room. The woman showed no signs of moving on.

"Do you come here during lunchtime?" she persisted, her tongue rimming her lips, kohl-lined eyes dancing over him.

"Sometimes."

He came as often as he could make it, except when he was out of town or in court, but she didn't need to know that.

Zan heaved himself to his feet. "Have a nice workout," he said, grabbing his towel and heading for the weight room.

An hour later, showered and back in his business suit, Zan sat behind his huge mahogany desk, which he'd had refinished. It gave him great pleasure to sit behind the desk of a man he so admired, the grandfather who had raised him, a man he still adored although he had long passed on.

Zan had been placed in a foster home, abandoned by the father who'd abducted him. When all efforts to find his mother or family had proved fruitless he'd been put up for adoption. His adoptive parents, hardworking people, had died in a car accident, and his aging grandparents had taken on the task of raising him, instilling in him a need to get an education and be somebody.

His adoptive grandfather had had a difficult time of it, attending law school when only a few people of color did. But he'd persevered, thrived, and returned to the Hempstead area to help his people. He'd never been rich but he'd developed a reputation as an aggressive attorney with a caring soul, a rarity in the legal business. Those qualities had been passed on to Zan.

Zan hit the intercom button. Miriam had been at lunch when he returned.

She answered in her cheerful voice. "Yes, Zan?"

"Any messages?"

"Several."

"Read them to me."

And she did. There was none from the woman he'd hoped to hear from. By now Kristie Phillips should have called, and he wondered what was up with that.

He'd programmed her number into his cell phone. After he disconnected with Miriam, he pushed a button and tapped his loafer restlessly, waiting for the connection to go through.

His call immediately went into voice mail. He remembered Kristie mentioning that she taught special ed. His sympathy went out to her. It must be difficult interacting with children all day when your own son was missing.

Zan liked the tone of her voice, warm and upbeat as she completed the greeting. It sounded a far cry from the sobbing woman who'd come to his office stressed and distressed. This must be the real Kristie Phillips, he thought as he waited for the beep.

"Hello. Timothy Zan McManus here. Zan if you prefer. Kristie, please call me so that we can continue our discussion. We need to move quickly if we're to find your son." He hung up after leaving his number.

There was a knock on his closed office door.

"Come in," Zan said, removing a file from his in-box and beginning the process of prepping for an upcoming case.

"Your three o'clock is here," Miriam said, politely.

He looked at her blankly. He didn't recall having an afternoon appointment.

"The father whose wife disappeared with his kids. The ex-wife moved in with her lover and took the kids with her."

"Yes. Yes, of course."

The man had been a walk-in. He'd been a pleasant surprise. He'd had the means and wherewithal to pursue his case aggressively. Zan had immediately taken him on.

Zan reached for the man's file, flipping through it idly. "Ah, yes, show Mr. Applebaum in."

"Will do. He's on his way." She bustled out.

He cleared his throat, attempting to stop her. "Uh, by the way, if Kristie Phillips should call, put her through."

Miriam blinked at him, obviously surprised. "Even if Mr. Applebaum is still with you?"

"Even if he is. Speaking with her will only take a minute."

"Okay," Miriam said, departing, lips pursed, eyebrows raised sky-high.

Zan glanced through Applebaum's file and stood, prepared to meet his client. But Kristie Phillips and her predicament remained on his mind. No man could possibly forget that heart-shaped face and those soul-searching amber eyes. They left an indelible imprint on your mind.

"Thank you, Lord," Lizette Stokes said when the school bell rang, ending sessions for that day.

Kristie watched the children's faces brighten. The volume certainly rose as they bounded for the exit and toward waiting parents. The school was a converted Tudor-style home in Merrick, Long Island, with a tremendous backyard. It was a ten-to-fifteen-minute drive from Kristie's home in Baldwin, depending on traffic.

A little hand tugged on her denim overalls. "Miss Phillips, do you think my mom will come to get me on time today?"

A cherubic face peered up at Kristie. Ian was being raised by his mother. She worked in Manhattan and more often than not arrived late to pick him up. He was usually the only child left, long after his classmates had gone home. Kristie felt sorry for both the little boy and his mother, who was working her fingers to the bone to provide him a home and the attention a dyslexic child needed. She'd bonded with her students, since classes at the Learning Center were small and no teacher was responsible for more than eight kids at any time.

Kristie liked getting to know her kids intimately. She liked working hands-on with the children and

getting to know the parents as people. Private education didn't come cheaply, but amazingly the students came from all walks of life. Most parents
would do almost anything to ensure that their kids
had a fighting chance before they were assimilated
into the public school system, certainly a less expensive way to go.

Kristie stroked Ian's wiry blond curls. He was
the by-product of interracial mating, not that it
mattered to her; a child was a child.

"Your mother will be here as soon as she can,"
she reassured the boy, swinging him up into her
arms and kissing his downy cheek. He smelled of
the candied apples they'd been making.

Ian wrapped his arms around her. "She takes so
long and I'm tired," he whined.

"Tell you what. We'll color while we wait for her,"
Kristie said, setting Ian down.

"Goodie." Ian skipped off to tell other children
who waited for parents who hadn't yet shown up.

Lizette rolled her eyes and mouthed, "You're
spoiling that boy."

"He deserves spoiling," Kristie said, fetching coloring books and crayons and distributing them
amongst the children.

She'd taken special interest in Ian, who reminded
her of her own little boy in so many ways. He was
bright but required patience and lots of loving.
She had an abundance of both.

With the kids hunched over tables, chatting and
coloring, Kristie took the seat next to Lizette and
prepared for the questions that would inevitably
come.

"What's going on?" her friend asked. "Have

you heard from Zan McManus since your last meeting?"

Kristie had failed to mention that the attorney had phoned to find out if she had gotten home okay. She didn't want Lizette making a big deal over his courteous inquiry. She'd meant to call Zan but had been trying to figure out how to come up with a retainer if he required one. Sure he'd told her not to worry about it, but as much as she wanted her child back she hated to accept charity, desperate as she was.

"I'm trying to figure out where I can get the money to pay Zan," Kristie said honestly. "I was thinking of cashing in my 401K, not that I have that much money saved."

"It's the only money you have," Lizette reminded her as if she needed reminding.

The private school offered its teachers a retirement plan, adding fifty cents for each dollar an employee saved.

Kristie shrugged. "My child is more important than any retirement plan. I'll take on a second job if it comes down to it."

"Like you have time," Lizette scoffed. "You're here a minimum of ten hours a day. Better to call Zan McManus and plead your case. He accepts pro bono cases or Paula would never have recommended him."

"I'd prefer not to do that," Kristie answered, though common sense dictated she put her pride aside. The longer Curtis was gone, the less likely she was to find him. Earl was not gainfully employed and had no particular ties to Long Island; therefore he could be anywhere. Kristie had forced him to move to Long Island when her ailing parents needed her. They had since passed on.

The small sum of money that had been her inheritance had been used up for day-to-day living, but she'd set a small amount aside for Curtis's education, and that plus her 401K might be enough to retain T. Zan McManus.

Kristie brightened visibly and reached for her cell phone. A little envelope indicated there were messages waiting. Excusing herself, she accessed the messages. The first was from her sister, Mikaela, who lived in New Jersey, the second from T. Zan himself. She felt herself grow warm as his gritty voice filled her ear. Kristie disconnected and put the phone away. She'd call him later when she got home, with Lizette out of the way.

"Someone must have left you a nice message," Lizette said, her voice taking on that knowing syrupy tone. "You're beaming. I haven't seen you smile in a while; I mean really smile, except at the children."

"Zan called," Kristie admitted, knowing there would be no rest for the weary if she simply ignored Lizette's question.

"So call him back."

"Later," Kristie said, hurrying off. "Mrs. Bennidetto is here to collect Wendy and I think I hear the Cohens' housekeeper coming. She usually drags her feet."

Conversation was placed on hold as they gathered the children's personal items, then greeted the parents and baby-sitters. Predictably, Ian was the only one left. He sat in a corner, sucking his thumb, holding back huge, unshed tears.

"Come here, baby," Kristie said, holding out her arms to him.

The little boy practically raced to their haven. Kristie rocked him back and forth as loud sobs wracked his plump body.

"Ian, your mom will be here soon. Has she ever not come for you?"

Ian sniveled. "No, Miss Kristie, but she's always late. When I get home it's dark and my friends are having their supper. I never get to play with them."

"But you get to play with the other kids here," Kristie said gently, setting the child back on his feet. "You get to help me take care of them. What would I do if I didn't have your help? Don't you know I need you, Ian?"

"You need me, Miss Kristie?" he asked, his eyes lighting up. He accepted the tissue Kristie handed him and proceeded to blow.

"I'm taking off," Lizette said, gathering her purse and the file with tomorrow's lesson plan. "Will you be okay by yourself?"

Kristie nodded at her over the top of Ian's head. "The security guard never leaves until I do."

"That's because he has the hots for you," Lizette said, winking.

"What's hots, Miss Kristie?"

Kristie glared at Lizette but softened her expression when Ian's mother rushed in. Lizette decided against leaving and waited for Kristie to gather the child's things.

"I'm terribly sorry, Ms. Phillips," the tired mother said. "The train broke down and we sat on the track for what seemed like hours. I came as quickly as I could."

Ian was off like a rocket, hugging his mother around the knees. "Hi, Mama. I was a good boy. So now can I have some candy?"

Melissa Goodman stroked her son's hair and hugged the child to her.

"It's okay," Kristie assured the harried parent. "Ian helped me with the children as he usually does. He's a good boy."

"Yes, I know, the best." Melissa hugged her son even more tightly.

Ian was on a high, his sulking forgotten.

Kristie waved good-bye to mother and child, picked up her purse, and prepared to join Lizette.

"Do you have plans?" Lizette asked when they were out in the parking lot. As if she didn't know that Kristie was going home to a silent house and a long tear-filled night.

"Yes, right," Kristie answered, "I'm going out ballroom dancing." She softened her tone. "I plan on calling every single person that Curtis and I know."

"Feel like company?"

"Would love company. Come over. I'll throw a salad or something together and we can have wine. I've got bottles left over from Christmas."

"You're turning into a lush," Lizette joked, as they got into their respective cars.

Kristie was glad for Lizette's company. As usual, a long, panic-filled night lay ahead. She would call Zan tomorrow or later, depending on when Lizette left.

Kristie led the way down Merrick Avenue and idled when her friend missed the light. Eventually they turned onto her block. She spotted the police car in front of her house and two plainclothes cops at her door. With heart racing and a dry mouth, she zoomed into her driveway, threw the car into park, and leapt out.

"Is there a problem, Officer?" she asked, while her heart invaded her throat. "Has my son been found?"

"Let's go inside, Mrs. Phillips," the shorter of them said, flashing his badge and confirming his legitimacy.

It was worse than she expected or why would they need privacy to speak to her?

Lizette's car screeched to a halt behind the policemen's vehicle. She flew from the driver's seat and bounded across the small front lawn.

"Are you okay? What's happening?"

Kristie began hyperventilating. Her throat had closed down and little pinpoints of light flashed before her eyes.

"Are you her friend?" the taller cop asked Lizette.

"Yes, I'm her friend."

"Let's get Mrs. Phillips into the house."

"Ms. Phillips," Kristie managed as the earth rose up to meet her and the shrubbery wavered back and forth.

Lizette took Kristie's purse, dug through it, and found the house keys. She let them in and keeping a firm hold on Kristie's elbow forced her to sit down.

"I'm getting you water," Lizette said, departing for the kitchen.

The cops remained standing in the small living room, waiting while Kristie took several gulps of ice-cold water. She had to maintain control now, until she heard what they had to say.

"All right, Officers, why are you here?" Kristie asked when she'd managed to get her breath back.

"You filed a missing person's report three days ago," the shorter one said gravely. "We're here to tell you that your husband's vehicle was found at John F. Kennedy Airport's parking lot."

The living room ebbed and flowed, then settled down. "Ex-husband," Kristie corrected in a tinny voice that was foreign to her ears. "Have you found my son, Officer . . ."

"Banks," the shorter filled in. "My partner's Officer Sloan."

Sloan shrugged. "We found a child's sneaker in the lot not too far from your ex's Honda." He held up what looked like a zip-lock bag, opened it, and removed Curtis's shoe.

"Oh, no," Kristie screamed, her hands flying to her chest, eyes Ping-Ponging out of her head. She took several painful breaths while Lizette sat next to her holding her hand, squeezing it tightly.

"Do you recognize the shoe?"

"It's Curtis's," Kristie said hoarsely. "What does finding it mean?"

"No point in speculating," Officer Banks interjected. "Could mean anything. Your husband might have been rushing to catch a plane. Your son's shoe might have fallen off if he was carrying him. Anything could have happened."

"You think Curtis has been taken out of the country?" Kristie said woodenly.

"What we think," Sloan said smoothly, "is that your ex and son were hurrying off somewhere. The fact that his car was parked at the airport seems to indicate he had a flight to catch. What we'll need to do is check the flight records of several carriers. Did he have relatives out of town?"

Kristie thought of the parents that Earl seldom spoke to. They lived in Arizona. She'd called them when Curtis and Earl had first gone missing, but they'd said they hadn't heard from Earl and had promised to call if they did. Earl and his parents had never been on good terms. Kristie guessed they'd seen him for what he was: a user of people and an escapist from the real world, burying his misery in booze and pills.

Kristie told the cops about Earl's parents and where they resided, confirming that she had already been in touch.

"What about siblings? Was your ex close to any of his brothers and sisters?"

"Not particularly."

Earl had a brother in the army overseas and a sister who lived the high life in Connecticut. Her husband was a successful mortgage banker. She'd made it clear she wanted nothing to do with Earl. He was an embarrassment and would only serve to upset her tidy little life.

"So where do we go from here?" Lizette asked Officer Sloan, whom she was eyeing and seemed to like.

He was eyeing her right back and Kristie was able to discern that there was no ring visible on his left hand.

"We check the flight records as mentioned, though that might take some time. The police in the surrounding states are already alerted. We did that the minute we confirmed your child and ex were missing. We'll probably have to engage the FBI's help if this drags on."

Lizette tugged on Kristie's shirtsleeve. "You know what I think, hon? You need to get on the phone this minute and call your attorney."

"Ms. Phillips has an attorney?" Banks asked, slyly. "Why would she need one? It's not like she's a suspect in her own son's disappearance."

"Are you just about done?" Lizette asked, standing and indicating clearly that the inquisition had ended.

"We're done for now, but we'll be in touch," Sloan said, his eyes drifting over Lizette's ample form. "You have a number where we can reach you," he asked, "in case Ms. Phillips is unreachable?"

Lizette removed her business card from the bag she'd thrown on the couch, scribbled her home number, and handed it to Sloan.

He scrutinized it carefully and after a while said, "A pleasure meeting you, Ms. Stokes." He eased his partner toward the door. "Do you live nearby?"

Kristie wondered what that was about. Why would the officer care where her friend lived?

"*Miss* Stokes," Lizette corrected, "and that depends on how you classify nearby. I live in Malverne."

Sloan had the audacity to turn back and wink at her. "I like that you're a miss," he said. "You'll be hearing from me."

After they'd left, Lizette handed Kristie the remote phone and insisted she dial Zan McManus.

Kristie held it, debating what she would say to him. She dug into her purse, found his card, and slowly began depressing the numbers. If ever she needed help, now was it.

Zan McManus stared out of his floor-to-ceiling windows and onto Long Island Sound. It was pitch-dark except for the lights from houses on the far shore. In the daylight it was a breathtaking view.

He was still amazed that he was able to afford all of this. Hard work and a wisely invested inheritance had gotten him here.

It had been a long day, one made longer by traffic. He'd just gotten home and his cellular phone still held no message from Kristie Phillips. He wondered why. The woman had seemed so gung-ho about getting her child back. He resisted the urge to call her again.

Pacing the length of his great room, Zan thought about getting on his computer and checking his e-mail messages, but he'd promised himself to leave work at the office. Even someone like him, with boundless energy, needed a break.

Zan's steps brought him to the kitchen and to the center island where he leaned a hip on the counter and debated. He'd had a late dinner with a female attorney friend, someone from his law school class. Terese was beautiful, bright, and quick-witted and they maintained a friendship based on harmless flirting.

Zan peeled himself off the counter, stuck his head in the refrigerator, and removed a bottle of spring water. He took a swig. The phone in the pocket of his sweatpants rang and he frowned. It was late for a client to be calling. Friends knew to call him at home after nine.

Zan glanced at the 516 number but didn't recognize it immediately. Although tempted to ignore the call, he punched the Talk button and grunted into it, "Hello." The person on the other end sounded as if she was gasping for air.

"Hello," Zan said louder, letting his irritability show. The thought occurred to him that it might be Kristie Phillips, and his voice softened.

"Kristie?" he inquired. "Is that you?"

"I-I-I'm sorry to bother you, Mr. McManus," her plaintive voice said. "It's j-j-just—"

"What's happened, Kristie? Take deep breaths and talk to me."

He could hear the air wheezing into her lungs as she strove to compose herself. Zan pressed his back against the refrigerator and began a series of leg flexes, waiting patiently for her to speak. He had this urge to take care of a woman he didn't even know. It baffled him.

"The police were here. They just left," she managed.

Zan was suddenly all business. "Why were they there? What did they want?"

"Earl's car was found at the airport along with one of my little boy's sneakers."

"Is foul play suspected?"

Zan could tell by Kristie's sharp intake of breath that he'd startled her.

"If they do, they never mentioned it. I need your help, Mr. McMan—"

"Zan."

"I don't have a lot of money except what I have in my 401K and what I've been saving for Curtis's education. If that's not enough, I'll rustle up some from somewhere. I'll do what it takes to find my boy."

The woman sounded like she was willing to prostitute herself. He didn't like that one bit.

"Didn't I tell you that we would discuss payment at another time?" Zan said brusquely. "How did you leave it with the police?"

Kristie told him about their suspicions and that flight records were being checked.

"Do you have any idea where your ex-husband

would have gone? Does he have friends or relatives in another state or country?"

Kristie told Zan about the severed relationship between Earl and his parents, about the brother in the army overseas, and about the sister who wanted nothing to do with him.

"Families have a way of pulling together when adversity hits," Zan said, speaking from experience. "Is there any possibility that Earl may have decided to visit his brother in Germany and taken Curtis with him?" Zan heard Kristie's gasp.

"Where would he get that kind of money?"

"Possibly his brother paid for the tickets. Does Curtis have a passport?"

"Yes. I applied for one because I was thinking of taking him on a vacation this summer."

The sobs that Kristie had been holding in turned to full-fledged wails. He felt for her. A woman in the background was saying something soothing. Zan wondered if she was a relative. How long would it take to get from his place to hers? She lived on the south shore, a good forty minutes away. *Get a grip.* It wasn't his place to comfort her. Besides, it sounded as if she already had emotional support. But he still felt helpless. The woman was hurting and he could do little about it tonight.

"What's your schedule like tomorrow?" he asked impulsively.

"I'm working," Kristie said through intermittent sobs.

"How about having lunch with me and coming up with a plan of action?"

"I don't have much time for lunch. I eat with the children."

He remembered she taught school, special ed.

"Dinner then?" Zan asked, and could promptly kick himself. What had gotten into him? What if she thought he was asking her out?

It's a business dinner, a little voice reminded him.

He could almost feel Kristie's hesitation coming at him in palpable waves through the earpiece.

Zan put on his T. Zan McManus voice, the one that brooked no nonsense and that he used to cross-examine witnesses.

"Kristie, you need me and I'm willing to help, but we need to sit down and plan a strategy. We can't do that if you don't trust me. What's the address of your school?"

He could hear the soft voice of the woman in the background say, "Give it to him."

Zan wondered if she was listening on another line. After several seconds went by, Kristie gave him the address of her school and Zan disconnected.

He rested his forehead against the cool surface of the refrigerator and closed his eyes. Outside, the waves beat an erratic symphony against the rocks. Finding Curtis Leone was going to be a challenge, especially if he'd been taken out of the country.

Zan loved a good challenge; it got his adrenaline pumping. And he would do almost anything to see Kristie Phillips smile again. He guessed she had a beautiful smile. What would it take to have her smile for him?

Chapter 3

It wasn't the first time that Earl had regretted his impulsive action. But what choice had Kristie left him? Curtis was a handful, requiring constant time and attention. Time and attention Earl did not have. The rambunctious six-year-old continually whined for his mother, demanding to be entertained.

The small Mexican village where they'd established temporary residence was quaint. Struggling American artists had come here to escape and it was more of an artisan colony than the typical tourist resort. Earl and Curtis blended with the population that was mostly bohemian, although they were the only African-Americans around.

Earl had rented a room from a Mexican woman who clearly needed the money. He'd posed as a widower who needed a place to regroup and unwind. He'd sold everything he had prior to leaving the United States, not that what he had was much.

But sales from his meager furniture and stereo system had gotten him here. He would need to pick up something fast or his rapidly dwindling funds would be gone. He had always been handy, so with the permission of his landlady he placed a sign in the window that he was a handyman.

Earl had soon found out that the tranquil little village had a seedier side. Drugs were cheap and plentiful and the artistic community used them to fuel the creative process. He would have no problem feeding his habit, provided he was willing to pay.

"Dad, when are we going home?" Curtis cried, repeatedly. The kid trailed his sneakered feet in the dirt. Earl had been forced to purchase the child a new pair of shoes to make up for the one that was lost when they were hurrying to catch the plane. They made their way up the main thoroughfare, stopping to examine the wares on display.

"Soon," Earl said gruffly, keeping an eye out for anyone who looked like they might sell drugs. He'd heard several of the expatriates made a living supplying their countrymen with marijuana and pills. Earl desperately craved a hit of the cloyingly sweet substance that helped keep him sane.

"I want to go home," Curtis repeated. "I want my mom."

"Shush. I'll take you back soon."

"That's a fine-looking boy you have," a potter said as Earl slowed to admire her craft. "How old is he?"

"Six," Earl answered shortly, keeping the conversation brief and volunteering no further information. He was no longer in the United States but one couldn't be too careful. Satellite TV made the world small.

"I'm hungry, Dad," Curtis whined, rubbing his tummy through the grimy T-shirt that he'd worn since he got there.

They'd need to do laundry shortly or make arrangements to have their wash done. While service was cheap here, it still cost money, money that he really didn't have. Earl spotted a gaunt-looking American with long greasy hair; he looked like the man he'd been told was a supplier. He was heading his way.

"Hey, Curtis," Earl said, removing a handful of pesos and thrusting them at his son. "Here. Go across the street and buy us a couple of tacos from that stand. Be careful."

Curtis's face creased into a smile. "Yes, Dad." He pocketed the money and skipped across the street, heading toward the stand with the bright red umbrella. Earl quickly began walking toward the man that he'd been told was a dealer, and could get him anything he wanted. The transaction would have to be completed quickly before his son's return. He would then send Curtis off on another errand, find a quiet alleyway, and take a quick hit.

What he really wanted was something more potent that would help him forget that his wife no longer wanted him. But he couldn't risk it. His money supply was low and he had the added responsibility of a small child. Taking Curtis was his own doing, but he'd wanted Kristie to feel the same pain she'd inflicted when she'd tossed him away.

Abducting Curtis was payback. Who did his ex-wife think she was, dumping him, now that she was a hoity-toity schoolteacher and self-sufficient?

"Hey, man," Earl greeted as the drug dealer approached.

The man eyed him warily. "What's up, bro?"

The dealer knew the lingo all right. His eyes slid over Earl, assessing him.

"What you got for me?" Earl asked as the man hefted the backpack he'd slung over a shoulder.

"That depends."

"I'm looking to score a half ounce or so," Earl said, removing a wad from his pocket and quickly counting out bills. From the corner of his eye he could see that Curtis had completed his transaction. The kid was about to cross the street. "My boy's coming," he said to the dealer. "I'll catch up with you. Where can we meet?"

The dealer pointed up the street to a store that sold cigars and smoking-related items, a head shop.

"In front of that store. Don't bring your kid."

"I won't."

Earl thought quickly. He needed to find something that would keep Curtis occupied and out of his hair for a few minutes. He could use a hit badly. On their way here they'd passed a park where a handful of mostly Mexican kids were playing soccer. Maybe he could persuade Curtis to join the children once his taco was eaten.

"Give me ten minutes," Earl said, walking toward Curtis.

"Ten minutes it is, not a minute longer. I have people to see, places to go."

"Daddy, Daddy," Curtis said, spotting his father

and running across the street right in front of a scooter.

"Curtis, watch out!" Earl shouted as his son narrowly missed being run over.

The teenager swerved, screaming foul expletives in a rapid torrent of Spanish.

Earl rushed into the street and grabbed his son around his waist, hoisting him onto his shoulders.

"You irresponsible son of a bitch!" he shouted at the teenager who'd righted his bike and was preparing to take off.

Another rapid outpour of Spanish followed, capturing the attention of nearby pedestrians. The last thing Earl needed was to be a sideshow. He couldn't risk it. Glaring at the teenager, he set Curtis down on the sidewalk.

The child had lost his tacos and began to wail. Damn it, there went more money down the drain. He'd have to shut him up.

"I'll buy you another," Earl promised, hurrying the boy across the street. He purchased two more tacos, then took Curtis to the park. Several of the children kicking a ball around appeared to have a good command of English, some even looked American. After skillful negotiating, Earl convinced them to let his boy join their game.

Curtis was a fairly decent soccer player and in just a few minutes he became an enthusiastic and popular participant. Earl signaled to the child that he would be back and retraced his steps.

The dealer was in the midst of another transaction when Earl approached. He hung back and waited his turn. Upon completion of his business, the man beckoned Earl with a slight tilt of his chin.

They began walking together. Money changed hands. Earl got his stash and was a happy man.

He found a deserted alleyway, removed the pipe he kept in his pocket, and filled it with weed. He ignited the bowl and took several tokes, inhaling the pungently sweet substance, and letting it take control. Already the sky looked bluer and every sense was enhanced. He felt as if he could walk on water, grow wings, and dance. It was a good stash. Gr-r-reat.

Earl tamped down the residue and shook it out onto the dirt. He leaned his back against a brick wall and contemplated his life: a life that could be simple, uncomplicated, and carefree. Pesos went far in this part of the world. If Kristie would join him they could have a helluva time.

In some vague part of his mind Earl remembered the child he had abandoned and made a conscious effort to pull himself together. The pot had made him thirsty and a beer would go down easy. He'd grab a quick one before he picked Curtis up.

The boy had seemed happy to be playing with others his age. It wasn't as if he'd been left alone. Several parents had been supervising the game.

One beer led to another and another, and before Earl realized it the time had gotten away from him. It was getting dark. When he returned to the park the soccer game had ended and Curtis was gone. Momentary panic set in and Earl's stomach lurched. What to do now?

He couldn't afford to lose the child; he was the only card Earl had left in his complicated game to get Kristie back. He couldn't exactly walk into a police station and tell the cops that he'd lost his son; it would only send up a red flag.

"Hey, amigo," a ragged-looking beggar greeted as Earl exited the park. "You got a peso or two?"

The man looked Mexican but obviously spoke English well. It was well worth asking some questions. "I'll give you money in return for your help."

"Anything, amigo."

"I'm looking for my son."

"A little boy about this high?" The man held his hand up, indicating Curtis's height.

"Yes, he's six years old. Dark skin like me. Missing tooth."

"Left the park with two gringos," the beggar said, his hand still held out.

"Where were they heading?"

He shrugged. "Don't know, amigo. I told you what I know. Now give me the money."

Earl shook a couple of pesos into the man's hand. The beggar stared at him. "You gotta be kidding," he sneered. "What am I supposed to do with this? Not enough here for *Cerveza*."

"That's all I got. Take it or leave it. Point me in the direction they were heading, I'll give you more."

The vagrant pointed a vague finger to the left. Earl had the feeling that was all he would get out of him. He might be lying but it was worth the additional coin he flipped into the man's open palm. He walked away, leaving the beggar grumbling about "el cheapo" Americans.

The side street Earl came to was unfamiliar. Several shops sported ABIERTO signs, and restaurants prepared to serve dinner. By now Earl was painfully straight, the effects of the pot and drinks having worn off. He wanted to kill Curtis. The kid should have sat down on a bench and waited until he came to get him. Now he had little choice but to stop passersby and ask if they'd seen a little black boy with two white adults.

Earl's first two inquiries met with blank stares until he found a couple who were bilingual and willing to help. They accompanied him into a sidewalk café and started up a conversation in rapid Spanish with a waiter, leaving Earl totally lost.

"Your son was here about half an hour ago," the male said, translating. "He came in with gringos and a white boy. The waiter assumed the children were friends."

"Did he see where they were heading when they left?" Earl asked.

The male again began quizzing the waiter and another rapid conversation ensued.

His new acquaintance translated. "Gustavo overheard them say they were going back to their hotel. They mentioned something about calling the police."

Earl began to sweat. One of his hands swiped his forehead. The police was just what he needed.

"Which hotel were they staying at?" he managed to ask. "Can I walk to it?"

The man gave him a curious glance and after more conversation with the waiter provided a name.

"It's a short taxi ride away," he said, "but a long walk."

Earl thanked the couple. Now he would be forced to shell out more money to get his child. Curtis was talkative. Who knew what he'd already said to the couple? Just wait until he got hold of that boy.

Earl wanted to bang his head against the concrete walls of the restaurant building. He was estupido. Stupid for leaving Curtis alone.

"Good luck to you," the man's wife said, touching Earl gently on the arm. Her husband helped him hail a battered Volkswagen cab and Earl climbed into it.

"Villa Rosa," Earl told the cabdriver, hoping that his lack of Spanish was not evident.

The cabbie nodded and took off in a cloud of billowing smoke. Forty minutes and the equivalent of twenty-five dollars later, they were still driving.

"Villa Rosa," Earl said between tightly clenched teeth.

"Another five minutes," the driver said, holding up the fingers of one hand.

Clearly Earl was getting the runaround. The driver knew he was foreign and wanted to build up his fare. But he didn't know whom he was playing with. Desperate times required desperate measures. He was about to get the surprise of his life.

Ten minutes and another five dollars later, they screeched to a stop in front of a boutique hotel covered in red bougainvillea.

"Thirty dollars," the taxi driver demanded, turning and holding his hand out.

Earl hopped out of the car, flashed a disarming smile, and said, "Got to get the money from the wife. She's inside. Wait here."

He disappeared into the bowels of the building, having no imminent plans to return.

*   *   *

Curtis rubbed his eyes. He was getting sleepy. As
much fun as his new friend Kevin was, it was time
to go home. Not home to the house where they were
staying, but home to Baldwin, New York, where he
and his mother lived.

Curtis missed his mom, but his dad had said
that she was too busy to take care of him. That's
why they were taking this vacation. His dad wasn't
as strict as his mom, and pretty much let him do
anything he wanted. He got to eat junk food, stay
up late, and watch the English channel on TV
while his father sat in a chair drinking beer. When
bedtime rolled around, his dad talked funny, and
sometimes he tripped over stuff on the floor and
Curtis helped him up.

"How are you holding up, champ?" the man
who'd introduced himself as Kevin's father, Mr. Martin, asked, while Kevin's mother fluttered around
the lobby of the hotel like a nervous bird, talking
to people.

"I'm sleepy," Curtis admitted.

"Yes, I know," Mr. Martin said, ruffling his hair.
"Your dad should show up shortly. We left our address with the shopkeepers in the area. He's probably looking for you."

Curtis wasn't hungry, because the Martins had
fed him dinner in the hotel's restaurant. It had been
the best dinner he'd had since leaving New York.
He'd even had ice cream and he and Kevin had
played an electronic game afterward.

Mrs. Martin was back at her husband's side and
Curtis heard the word "police" mentioned. He knew
it was a bad word because his father hated it. Kevin's
mother was now complaining in a whiny voice.

"Curtis's father's just plain irresponsible. Who in their right mind would leave a six-year-old kid all by himself in a park in Mexico?"

"Keep your voice down, he'll hear you," Mr. Martin hissed while his wife rolled her eyes.

Kevin was sitting on a chair beside Curtis, his legs stretched out. They were both worn out from the soccer game.

"So what do we do now?" Mrs. Martin screeched. "Wait here all night? What if the father never shows up? What are we supposed to do with this child?"

His dad better show up. He liked the Martins but he really didn't know them and he didn't like the idea of sharing a bed with Kevin. He had smelly feet. Curtis had noticed this when Kevin had taken his sneakers off.

The word "police" was mentioned again, and Curtis shivered. His father would not like that at all. He'd punish him good if these nice people turned him over to the cops as Mrs. Martin kept threatening.

Just then, Curtis spotted his father, rushing through the lobby, as if Pobrecito, the dog at the boardinghouse, were chasing him. He was wild-eyed and dirty, even dirtier than Curtis, who'd fallen a few times while chasing the ball.

Curtis was up like a shot, bounding across brown tile floors and waving his arms wildly to get his father's attention.

"Daddy, Daddy!"

A huge smile broke out on his father's face as he spotted Curtis. Then his expression changed to a nasty one and he wagged his finger at him.

"You have no idea the trouble you're in, young

man," Earl said, pressing the tip of his finger against Curtis's nose. "When I get your butt home you're a goner."

"Are you Curtis's father?" Mr. Martin approached. Mrs. Martin followed steps behind.

Curtis remembered his dad saying his mom was "a nag" when she behaved like Mrs. Martin. Sometimes he would slap her to shut her up.

"Yes, I am," Earl said, smiling. "Thanks for taking care of my boy."

He took Curtis's hand and began moving away.

"Hold on a moment," Mr. Martin called. "I'll need to see identification just to be sure."

Earl reached into his back pocket, then removed his hand. "Oh, my Lord," he said irritably. "My pocket's been picked." He began to pat the front of his jeans and the pocket of his T-shirt, looking for his wallet.

An angry man raced into the lobby, shouting at his dad in a mixture of English and a language Curtis did not understand.

"Hold up, amigo," the angry man said.

Earl looked like he wanted to run, but everybody in the lobby was staring at them.

"Cough up the *dinero,* hombre."

"Uh," Earl said, "I lost my wallet. Looks like one of your people robbed me."

Mr. Martin took out some money and began counting. "How much does he owe you?" he asked in a voice that wasn't friendly.

"Thirty U.S. dollars, plus tip."

"Highway robbery," Kevin's mother muttered, as her husband shoved some bills in the man's hand. The driver stomped off, clicking his teeth.

"I'll pay you back," Earl said to the Martins. "Write down your name and I'll leave the money at the front desk."

Mrs. Martin hurried toward a big desk and came back with paper and pen, which she shoved at Mr. Martin.

He scribbled down something and gave the paper to Earl. "Here."

"Thanks, man." They shook hands.

"Are you going to be okay?" Mr. Martin asked Curtis.

"Yes, sir. I just want to go home." He rubbed his eyes. He was very tired.

They left the hotel and walked down a dark street. When they turned the corner, Curtis's father whacked him on the behind.

"You cost me a lot of money today," he yelled. "What did you say to those people?"

Curtis couldn't remember. It had been a long day. He was tired and wanted to go home. This vacation wasn't fun as he'd been promised. He wanted to sleep in his own room and hug the stuffed dog he'd had since he was a baby.

"Answer me, boy," his father said, whacking him again.

This time it really hurt and Curtis sobbed. "I want to go home."

"I'll give you something to cry about, sissy," his father said.

It was times like this he hated his father. He'd hurt his mommy and made her cry too.

Chapter 4

"Did you bring pictures of Earl with you as I requested?" Zan asked. They'd chosen a restaurant in Freeport because of its convenience and were now seated on the outdoor deck.

"I don't have any, I destroyed them all," Kristie whispered, looking at him as if Earl's name were pure poison.

Her face had grown ashen and there were deep lines rimming her mouth. Zan could understand wanting to start your life afresh after a divorce, but surely she must have saved some photos of her ex, if for no other reason than to remind her little boy that he had a father.

Zan had never been married, but he'd once been engaged. The engagement had ended badly and he'd sworn off romance since. He'd consider marriage when it was time to have children. That gave him a full five years to play with since he didn't plan on marrying until he turned forty. He planned on finding a woman who was independent and had a life, one with no particular interest in his business affairs. He wanted someone who was different from Kristie Phillips, though her vulnerability held a certain appeal.

"What about photos of your boy? You must have some," he said, carefully.

Kristie seemed like the type of woman who would definitely have pictures of her child. She might even carry a few in the purse she hugged so tightly as if substituting it for the son that was missing.

Kristie's eyes lit up. "Of course I do. I never leave home without pictures of Curtis."

As he suspected, she dug through the cavernous purse and extracted a large white envelope. "I had these taken at Sears the week before . . . well, the week before Curtis disappeared." She slid the envelope his way.

Zan stuck out his hand, halting the envelope's progress. He saved it from sliding into the murky water below them.

Kristie's eyes almost popped out of their sockets when she realized what she'd almost done. One hand flew to her open mouth, the other reached across the table, grasping his arm around the cuff of his shirt.

He liked the feeling of her fingers against his bare wrist.

"Thanks for acting so quickly," she said. " I don't know what I would have done if those photos fell into the water. They're the most recent ones of Curtis."

The unshed tears in Kristie's eyes made him want to wrap his arms around her and hold that slender body against his. She looked so fragile he wondered if the breeze rippling the waters of the Woodcleft Canal might blow her away. They were in Guy Lombardo country, though the bandleader was long dead.

Kristie realizing that she still held his wrist captive removed her hand as if she'd been scorched. "I'm sorry. I'm wired, I guess."

"And have every reason to be. Drink your wine."

Zan found his horn-rimmed glasses and shoved them onto his nose. He was glad to have something to do to compose himself. Kristie Phillips was beginning to get under his skin. Her touch alone had triggered a reaction. She was his client; anything other than business could not be entertained. It would be unethical and imprudent of him especially since she wasn't what he was looking for.

Zan stared at Curtis's photo. Kristie's son was a cute little boy with a wide smile. He really didn't look like Kristie except for those eyes, eyes that were wide and held a glimmer of mischief. They sparkled with joy the same way his mother's did when she let her guard down and dared to hope.

A waitress tottered over to them in too-high heels. Zan wondered how the young woman in her twenties managed to carry a tray heaping with food and not lose her balance.

"Salads," she said, setting down their two plates.

Zan put aside the photographs and picked up his fork. "May I keep the photo? Bon appétit, by the way. Your kid is cute. Does he look like his father?" He wondered if his comment would elicit a strong reaction.

"Yes, he does," Kristie said matter-of-factly. "And yes, you may hold on to the picture."

"The next step is to hire a private detective," Zan said, shoveling salad into his mouth.

"How much will that cost?"

Kristie paused, waiting breathlessly for his answer. Money was obviously a big concern for her.

"Didn't I say we would work something out?"

"I won't accept charity," Kristie said clearly but quietly.

Zan admired that she wasn't looking for a handout. They needed to hire a private eye and soon if they were to stand a chance of finding her kid. The police could only do so much, as they were overburdened with cases like these. Curtis Leone was another missing child of the thousands that disappeared each year.

"Tell you what," Zan said. "How about we work out an agreement? You can pay me over time."

"We'll need to get it written down and I'll sign," Kristie said, picking at her salad.

"As you wish. I'll have Miriam mail you an agreement." He'd decided if that's what it took to get her to agree, so be it. "I have homework for you," he said, watching her startled expression. "Find me a photograph of Earl and gather the phone numbers and addresses of family and friends, anyone who knew Earl well."

Kristie nodded. "I'll try."

"Make it a priority."

The waitress arrived with their entrées, and the conversation shifted. Zan wanted to know why she'd chosen special ed as a career.

"My older sister had a learning disability," Kristie

admitted. "She'd study and study but her grades were always bad. My parents thought she was lazy; then they had her tested and learned she had a hearing impairment."

"So what did they do?" Zan asked, liking the sound of her voice as she told the story.

"They sent her to therapy. Mikaela isn't totally deaf but she's able to read lips effectively. Once the problem was identified, her grades immediately improved. It was her experience that made me realize how a normally bright child could get lost in the system. When teachers are uncaring or overburdened with students, a child with special needs gets overlooked."

Kristie's insight and compassion touched Zan in a hidden place. Had it not been for the McManuses he wouldn't be where he was today. He would have been just another statistic lost to foster care. Zan could barely read when he'd been adopted. It had taken a lot of effort on his adoptive parents' part to get an eight-year-old up to third grade standards.

"You're a very caring person, Kristie Phillips," Zan said, sitting back and watching her blush.

"That might be so, but I'm keeping you from getting home." She began fumbling in her bag and he realized she was trying to find money to pay her share.

"The treat's mine," Zan said, reaching for his wallet and signaling the waitress at the same time.

A couple with two young children entered and were seated. Kristie gave them a longing look.

"Sure I can't persuade you to have dessert?" he asked, hoping to distract her.

"No, thanks."

Zan didn't want the evening to end, but he had a trial the next day and he needed to go home and prepare. He took care of the bill and helped Kristie from her chair. Then holding her by the elbow he escorted her out to the beat-up Toyota that looked like it might not make it home.

"Call me tomorrow," he said, as she slid those long legs of hers into the driver's side.

She nodded and waved. "I will."

"Drive safely," he couldn't help saying, as she prepared to pull out from the curb.

"You too."

The engine groaned as Kristie nailed the accelerator and took off.

He wondered why she seemed so anxious to get away from him.

Kristie thought about Zan McManus all the way home. He was the type of man she had hoped to meet when she was in her early twenties and still believed in Prince Charming. But she'd met Earl Leone first, who'd initially swept her off her feet with his liquid tongue and grandiose schemes. He was a talker and had big plans. What she hadn't found out until it was too late was that Earl was the one who needed to be taken care of. He needed someone to save him from himself. He was what you called codependent.

Kristie had made every excuse in the book for Earl. First she'd thought that he was bright but just needed direction. She'd also thought that he was overly affectionate rather than needy. Bad luck seemed to find Earl wherever he went, and she'd

COME BACK TO ME

attributed his misfortune to a tough life growing up with cold parents whose kids were an inconvenience.

When she learned that he liked to do drugs, she bought Earl's excuse that he needed something to help him relax. But when he graduated from grass to hallucinatory pills, Kristie realized the problem was serious. Earl's moods were mercurial and he couldn't keep a job. Kristie soon found that she was carrying most of the weight, while her husband, the big guy, lounged on the sofa. It was time to do something about him. Them.

Then Kristie got pregnant and having an abortion went against everything she believed. Earl first started hitting her in her sixth month of pregnancy. It started as slaps and soon became punches when she was too lethargic to prepare the huge meals he insisted on having. Never mind that eating wasn't a priority. Earl would rather do drugs.

She put up with his abuse, arguing that her child needed a father. But when it became evident that Earl had no intention of ever finding a job, and Curtis was of an age to realize his wasn't a happy home, she took action. It was an ugly experience and it took a full year to get Earl out of her house.

Kristie pulled into her driveway, wondering where the time had gone. She had no memory of the short drive from Freeport to Baldwin, but she did have total recall of her dinner with Zan. Why couldn't she have met someone like him when she was young?

As usual, inserting her key in the lock brought with it pangs of loneliness. Loneliness and an incredible pain. Normally Curtis, if he'd been entrusted to a baby-sitter's care, would come running, throwing his arms around her knees and sending her stumbling. She'd remove a treat from her bag and hand it to him. And he would act as if she'd given him gold.

There was no joyous laughter from her child as she entered, just an empty living room and the lamp that she'd left permanently on. It represented a beacon to welcome Curtis home. Kristie checked the machine for messages as had become her custom, hoping against all odds that she would hear Earl's voice, or better yet, her son's.

She had the usual assortment of calls, some from solicitors, others from concerned friends, and one from her sister, asking how she was holding up. The final message had no voice to it, just a resounding click while the phone was hung up. It made Kristie wonder who might have called.

She shrugged out of her clothes, got comfortable in sweats, and sitting cross-legged on the bed, returned Mikaela's phone call.

Her sister answered in a too-loud voice, a result of her hearing impairment.

"Kristie?"

Mikaela had obviously looked at her caller ID.

"I'm returning your call," Kristie said.

"How did it go?"

"Not bad. Pretty painless, though there were times I admit that I got a bit misty-eyed."

"To be expected," Mikaela said. "God, I don't know what I would do if Cara or Josh were missing. I'd probably be committed to a looney bin."

Cara and Josh were Mikaela's kids. They were ten and twelve and Mikaela devoted her life to them. She had left a lucrative job to become a homemaker. She wanted to see her kids grow up.

Kristie told her about the plan Zan had cooked up and that he wanted to enlist the services of a detective.

"A detective," Mikaela said. "Sounds like that's going to cost you a bundle. Do you need money? If you do I can loan you some. Ken won't mind."

Ken was Mikaela's husband, a successful marketing executive at one of the better-known advertising agencies.

It was nice of Mikaela to offer but Kristie planned to keep her gesture in reserve. She hated to borrow money, but accepting a loan from family was better than being beholden to a stranger, and Zan McManus was hardly a friend.

Kristie rang off, promising to come and visit Mikaela and her family at their place on the central Jersey shore as soon as it was possible.

The phone rang again and she reached for the receiver without bothering to check to see who was calling. She thought she heard a child's muffled voice before the phone was disconnected and quickly hit the Caller ID button to see who had called, but no number registered.

Sleep was the furthest thing from her mind now. Kristie used the remote to snap on the TV, hoping against all hope that the phone would ring again. This time she wouldn't be so quick to answer. This time she would wait and see if a number popped up.

She must have nodded off, because the next thing she remembered was being jolted awake by the newscaster's voice. She could swear that she'd heard her name mentioned. Now she would never know.

* * *

Lizette was out walking her dog, Pooch, when a Chevy Blazer idled to a stop. Pooch, an obnoxious pug that only she could love, started an angry yapping.

"Hush," Lizette said, though her heart slammed against her chest and her fingers curled around the mace she kept in her jeans pocket.

"Well, hello there," a deep male voice said from the dark interior.

She didn't recognize the vehicle. It wasn't one that belonged to her neighbors. What was a strange man doing, casing her block trying to pick her up?

"Remember me?" the man asked, sticking his head out of the driver's window.

Lizette squinted at him, trying to make out the dark form.

"Officer Sloan," the voice supplied. "I was driving by and thought I recognized you."

No one would just happen to be driving by her Malverne block, a primarily family neighborhood.

"Oh, Officer Sloan," Lizette said, batting her eyelashes at him. "Of course I remember you. You're hard to forget."

It was a crock. She was tossing him a line. He knew it and she knew it. Still Lizette couldn't resist flirting with the handsome officer who'd seemed to be interested in her.

"So what really brings you here?" she said as Pooch bared his teeth and began to snarl.

"You," Sloan said honestly. "I couldn't get you out of my mind. So I checked out the number you gave me and looked up the address. It's one of the bennies of working for the police department. You're privy to all sorts of interesting information."

"And exactly what types of things did you find out about me?" Lizette asked, glad that she hadn't bothered to change into her usual dog-walking attire and still wore her hip-hugging jeans and silk shirt.

"We can discuss that over dinner," Sloan said, slipping his long, lean body out of the SUV and approaching her.

"Don't get . . ." Lizette said, holding up a hand. But it was already too late. With a snarl and a growl, Pooch had attached himself to the policeman's pant cuff and showed no signs of letting go.

Sloan kicked out and Pooch's jaw locked more firmly around his ankle.

"Stop it this minute," Lizette cried. "Down, boy."

Pooch gave her his droopy-eyed look but seemed reluctant to let go. Officer Sloan shimmied from one foot to the other while the miserable little beast got an even better hold.

"All right, Pooch. Enough," Lizette yelled, smothering her laughter. Pooch had never bitten anyone, not as far as she could recall, but he was temperamental and Sloan was scared.

"Get off me," Sloan shouted, hopping about as if firecrackers had exploded under his feet. "Control your nasty little beast."

"My dog is not nasty," Lizette said as Pooch finally detached himself and skulked away. He took a seat at Lizette's heels, growling ominously.

"Hmmm," Sloan said, examining his ankle for damage. "That's a matter of opinion. Look what he did."

Lizette made out teeth marks but there was no hole in his slacks. She fixed Sloan with a steely-eyed glare. "My dog is extremely smart. He did what any self-respected pug would do if her mistress was accosted by a stranger at night."

"So now I've accosted you?" Sloan said, coming closer until Lizette could smell a very masculine cologne. Pooch let out another vicious growl.

For someone who claimed to have been passing through the neighborhood, Sloan was certainly decked out for a night on the town. Lizette's eyes roamed over him, liking his snakeskin cowboy boots and the way his jeans hugged his thighs. He was narrow-waisted, had broad shoulders, and his unbuttoned shirt exposed crisp chest hairs. Hairs that she wouldn't mind running her fingers through.

"Like what you see?" he asked, coming even closer. Pooch's snap at air caused him to jump nimbly back. "Keep that ferocious dog at bay."

Lizette bent over and scooped Pooch into her arms. The canine needed to go on a diet and soon. She stroked the dog's head, making little cooing noises. "Don't let that bad man frighten you."

"So what's a lovely thing like you doing out here alone?" Sloan leered.

"I'm hardly alone. I have Pooch," Lizette pointed out, as the dog continued to lurch at Sloan, flashing his jagged whites.

"You have a point. That's some bodyguard."

Lizette began to laugh. She was enjoying the policeman's dry humor. He was making no bones about his interest in her and she was very interested in him.

"So what about dinner?" Sloan asked as old Mr. Peterson came ambling down the sidewalk with his golden retriever on a leash.

"You tell me the time and place and I'll be there. I normally don't go out with strangers unless I know their first names."

"The name is Ed," Sloan said, giving her a smile designed to send the female heart into palpitations. "Is tomorrow night good?"

Lizette thought quickly. She had a dental appointment she would have to reschedule, but it wasn't an emergency, just a teeth cleaning.

"Tomorrow night's fine. Where shall we meet?"

"I'll pick you up."

She looked at him, startled. So he was bent on doing this the old-fashioned way. Who would have guessed?

"Good evening, Ms. Stokes," Mr. Peterson said as he cruised to a stop. "It's a fine night for dog walking, don't you think?" He eyed Ed Sloan curiously. Lizette knew that by tomorrow the entire block would know that she'd been seen on the sidewalk with "her new man."

Peterson's golden retriever did a little prance and Pooch squirmed in Lizette's arms, anxious to get down and nuzzle his friend. Lizette set the pug down and he wandered over to make nice to Peterson's dog.

"Seven o'clock then?" Ed said, sliding back into the Blazer. "Wear something nice."

"Where are we going?" Lizette asked.

"That's for me to know and you to find out. See you tomorrow."

"It's apartment Nine-C," Lizette shouted at him.

He wiggled his fingers and took off in a roar. "Till tomorrow then."

"New boyfriend?" Mr. Peterson asked, coughing

on the exhaust fumes that Ed's vehicle had left behind.

"Could be," Lizette answered. "I'm working on it. These days you don't know."

"Young people," Peterson muttered, continuing on his way, his reluctant retriever stumbling along beside him.

Pooch let out a high-pitched yelping as his friend walked away. Lizette thought maybe it was best to bring him in before he woke up the sleeping neighborhood. She was excited about her date. Ed Sloan could be useful. It would be good to have a friend in the police department, one with the inside scoop. Kristie needed any edge she could get, and Ed might provide just the edge she needed.

Chapter 5

"Can you believe Ed Sloan asked me out?" Lizette whispered as Kristie's path and hers crossed in the hallway. They were hustling to their respective classrooms.

"Why do you seem so surprised? The man has been salivating at you as if he were a dog in heat."

As upset as Kristie had been, she'd noticed. The lustful looks Officer Ed Sloan had been throwing Lizette's way could have been detected by a blind bulldog.

Lizette grimaced and drew her hands across her abundant hips. "It's not like I'm a sex symbol. The man could have anyone that he wanted."

"That's debatable. He obviously wants you. Personally, he does nothing for me, but then again I'm not looking."

"I think Ed Sloan is hotter than a firecracker," Lizette admitted.

Beauty was indeed in the eye of the beholder.

Kristie wished that her friend would stop putting herself down. Lizette was a little overweight but very attractive.

A voice came from behind them. "Break it up, ladies, and move along. You have children waiting."

They both smothered a grin as Constance St. George, the principal, clomped by in what she considered stylish heels.

"See you later," Lizette mouthed, sprinting down the hallway in a slinky getup more appropriate for a Manhattan nightclub than teaching school. Ed Sloan had obviously had an effect on her.

Kristie had slept poorly and couldn't resist yawning. She'd called the cable television station last night hoping that someone might tell her that what she thought she overheard wasn't a wishful dream. But no one had been able to help her. The program director was supposed to call back but who knew how long that would take? In the event that someone did return the call, she'd kept her cell on vibrate.

The day went by quickly and she'd almost forgotten she'd promised to phone Zan. As soon as the last child left she hopped into her car, got out her phone, and dialed his number. He was probably already gone from the office and she was reluctant to call his cell. Lizette wasn't around either. She'd left school early to prepare for her date.

"Zan McManus here," Zan's deep voice boomed at her.

What happened to the T? Kristie wondered. He'd probably been expecting a personal call, hence the informality. Anyone who looked like Zan must have oodles of girlfriends.

COME BACK TO ME

"This is Kristie Phillips," she said, awed by his tone.

"Oh, Kristie, hi. I was hoping to hear from you. How are you, hon?"

Hon? Zan's voice had changed, growing more warm and welcoming as he spoke.

"I'm okay, it's just been a busy day." She apologized for calling so late in the evening. "I had the strangest experience last night."

Kristie explained what she thought she'd heard.

"Hmmmm," Zan said. "It's definitely worth checking out, though it might have been one of those missing persons' updates. You know, the kind made popular by John Walsh, the one who lost his son Adam."

It could have been. The news had been on when she'd awakened and she'd made the assumption it was a newscast.

"I retained a detective," Zan said, "someone I trust. He's done work for me in the past and has an excellent reputation for ferreting out all sorts of interesting information."

Again, Kristie couldn't resist asking how much it would cost.

Zan sighed loudly. Her concerns were probably getting awfully old to him. "Bill Federick's a fair man," he finally said. "And you need him. He isn't bound by the same legal constraints as an attorney is. Do you have anything for me?"

Anything? Kristie remembered she'd promised to try to get him Earl's photo and the numbers and addresses of anyone Earl knew. She'd planned on collecting that information this evening when she got home.

"I'll get to it this weekend," Kristie promised, re-alizing she was probably holding him up from getting home.

"You can do better than that. The sooner you get me even one name, the sooner Bill can do his job. You do want to find Curtis, don't you, Kristie?"

Zan sounded skeptical as if he thought maybe she had changed her mind about wanting her son back. Curtis was her life, her soul, and the only thing that mattered in this whole crazy world. She told Zan that.

"Earl's parents' names are Benjamin and Tina. They live in Phoenix, Arizona, at 405 Tequesta Street," Kristie said.

"Tequesta? Sounds like a beer," Zan quipped, making her laugh.

She remembered then that she was probably holding him up. It was time to go home, lonely as home was. She'd let Zan get back to whatever he was doing.

"I'll get you more information as soon as I can," Kristie promised, sticking her key into the ignition and revving the engine.

"Make it soon," Zan countered.

"Tomorrow. I promise," Kristie responded impulsively. She'd just committed to going through whatever personal effects Earl had left behind tonight. She hoped she was up to it.

"Bring what you find to my office, or better yet, I'll come by your school. We'll have lunch."

Lunch? Had he forgotten she didn't have a full hour for lunch?

"I'll bring food to you," Zan said. "Surely you can take a half hour out to have a bite with me."

Assertive. Too confident. Zan was making her nervous.

Her attorney was taking a lot of interest in her and she didn't know what to make of it.

"Don't you have a busy day tomorrow?" Kristie queried. "What about trials? Work?"

"You are my work," Zan said in that gravelly voice designed to make shivers skitter up and down your spine.

She might be work but Zan certainly had cases that were more lucrative than hers. While he made her feel special, Zan McManus was probably the type of attorney that made all of his clients feel special. She shouldn't make too much of this.

Kristie drove off realizing she was much too interested in Zan. The only male that should be in her thoughts right now was Curtis.

"Wow! You look dynamite." Ed Sloan's long, low whistle made Lizette tingle all over.

Pooch growled at him and Lizette admonished the dog, "Stay. Thank you," she answered, wondering if the figure-clinging dress she'd crawled into made her hips look wide and her derriere like an overinflated tire. The look in Ed's eyes told her otherwise. He made her forget that she was considered a full-figure girl. It was obvious Ed liked what he saw.

"Ready?" he asked, jingling his car keys.

"Ready."

Lizette made sure Pooch was settled, locked her door, and entered the elevator. Inside, Ed took her hand and pressed the palm to his lips.

"I'm a lucky man," he said. "I'm going out with the most beautiful woman in Malverne." He gave the hand he was holding another moist kiss.

Ed was hardly chopped liver in the same snake boots as last night, except this time he wore them with black dress pants and a form-fitting T-shirt that showed off his pecs. An unzipped black leather bomber completed the look. It crossed Lizette's mind that he had combined the Russell Crowe, bad boy look, with that of the starving downtown artist. What was it he saw in her?

After twenty minutes of driving they ended up in Long Beach, a lovely waterfront community. The restaurant he'd chosen was packed with locals but he'd reserved a table for them. Ed seemed to know everyone there was to know, and the men came over to slap him on the back and inspect Lizette up close.

She looked around at the willowy women in tailored slacks and microminis, wondering how she could possibly compete with them. But Ed ignored the predatory women and seemed to have eyes only for her.

"How's your girlfriend?" he asked when Lizette sipped on wine and he slugged beer from the bottle.

"Are you talking about Kristie?"

"Yeah, she's the only one I know."

"Holding up. Kristie's brave. I don't how I would handle it if my son disappeared into thin air."

"Hmmm," Ed said, closing the menu and raising a skeptical eyebrow.

He was starting to annoy her. "What's hmmm supposed to mean?"

"You don't have kids, I take it?"

"I never married."

Ed let out a belly-splitting laugh. "The two don't necessarily go hand in hand."

"They do for me."

"You're a traditional girl. I like that," Ed said, taking the conversation in another direction. They talked about other things, ate their meal, and ordered cappuccinos.

"So how come you're still single?" Earl asked, leering at her.

He was a player but sweet. "I could ask you the same thing," Lizette tossed back. Her annoyance was over with and she was beginning to enjoy the repartee.

"I used to be married. It didn't work out." He didn't bother elaborating.

"You didn't have kids?"

"Thankfully, none."

A woman in her thirties, wearing too much make-up, galloped by their table, then slowed down. "Hi, Ed," she said, thrusting her chest out.

"Hey, Ronnie. How's it going?"

"Who's your friend?" she asked, staring at Lizette.

Ed was forced to make introductions. Lizette got the distinct impression that she was being sized up.

After Ronnie left she asked, "What's the story with her?"

"She's someone I used to date a long time ago."

Ed wasn't big on explanations. Lizette, deciding she had no claim on him, let it go.

While they downed Sambuca, Ed surprised her by asking, "Do you really believe Kristie's son just disappeared?"

Lizette couldn't imagine what he was getting at or even trying to say.

"What am I missing?" she asked.

Ed splayed his palms. "It just seems strange that your friend continues to function, go to work, have a normal life, when her kid could be anywhere."

"What's she supposed to do, die?" Lizette snapped, feeling the need to defend her friend. "Kristie's a survivor. She had to be. You have no idea what she's been through with that no-good ex-husband of hers. Outwardly she may be coping but inside she's a mess. Curtis is Kristie's entire life."

"Then how come she hasn't gone screaming to the newspapers and gotten publicity? How come she doesn't have flyers posted on the block, or all over Baldwin as a matter of fact? The more people that are made aware of a missing child, the more likely that child is to be found."

"Kristie's not a very public person," Lizette answered, astounded that Ed doubted that her friend wasn't devastated. "She doesn't like attention drawn to herself. She wants to go about her search quietly. That's why her attorney suggested hiring a private detective."

Ed's fingers plowed through cropped salt-and-pepper hair. "Why does your friend need an attorney? She's not a suspect. Getting a lawyer involved only hinders a police investigation. An attorney will protect Kristie's interest, not her child's."

Ed looked at her expectantly, awaiting her response. Lizette felt her blood begin to boil. Why was he interrogating her and taking jabs at Kristie? She wondered if this dinner invitation had simply been an excuse to pump her for information. She decided the best defense was an offense with him.

"You cops haven't been much help. It's been five days and the police have come up with zero." Lizette's thumb and index finger made an O.

Ed shrugged. "We're doing the best we can under the circumstances. Kristie Phillips's case isn't the only one we have."

"Obviously."

Lizette didn't like the way the evening was turning out. Ed Sloan, as attractive as he might be, was beginning to get on her nerves. She hated closedmindedness or linear thinkers. She yawned. Maybe he would get the hint and take her home.

"Tired?" Ed commented, picking up on her body language.

"Yes, it's been a long day."

"I'll take you home," he said, standing and waiting for her to do the same.

An evening that had begun with such promise had come to an end. Win some and lose some. A friendship like she had with Kristie was more valuable than anything Ed had to offer. If he wasn't in her friend's corner, then she had to let him go.

They drove back to her place in complete silence. When they arrived, Lizette thanked Ed for dinner and he surprised her by accompanying her to her door.

On the ninth floor, Ed held out his hand for her key. Still annoyed, Lizette gave it to him. He unlocked the apartment and stood back, waiting for her to enter.

"Night, Lizette," Ed said, his fingers stroking her upper arm. "I had a good time and hope you did too." Instead of zooming in for her lips as she'd expected, he kissed her cheek.

"I'll call you," he said, turning away, then turning back before entering the elevator. "Better yet, you call me."

Lizette didn't answer. Ed Sloan had pissed her off. She'd call him all right, when hell froze over.

Ryan Velox was an ambitious television newscaster who'd left a small town to try big city reporting. He'd accepted a position at a cable channel on Long Island, and the money, although not what he'd hoped for, was better than what he'd made previously.

He was bound and determined to make a name for himself in an industry that was competitive. Ryan had begun dating Janet, a woman who taught at the Learning Center. In passing she had mentioned Kristie Phillips's plight. It had gotten Ryan to thinking that maybe there was a story here.

Recently, there had been a lot in the news about missing children. Regretfully, many of these children later turned up dead, but there had been few follow-up stories about the families left behind, or how the loss had affected them.

Ryan remembered hearing about a child whose dad had abducted him and flown him to Saudi Arabia. It had taken months, actually years, for the mother to get her daughter back. Janet had mentioned an acquaintance, Paula, having a similar experience. It had piqued Ryan's interest.

Stories like these required research, but there were certainly enough faces posted on milk cartons to make it worthwhile, and there had to be a database listing missing children. If it came down to it he would ask for John Walsh's help. He was determined that his broadcast would get national attention. It would be a win-win situation all around. Ryan would get the promotion he deserved while providing a much-needed service.

Ryan's proposal so far had been greeted by his boss with enthusiasm. A couple of nights back he had deviated from his script and taken the liberty of mentioning Kristie Phillips's situation. Since then the television station had been flooded with calls and he'd been given the go-ahead to pursue stories like hers. To get Kristie to talk would require Janet's help.

Ryan picked up the phone and punched in Janet's number. She would most likely be in bed. He wished he could be there with her.

The answering machine clicked on and Ryan left a message. He'd call Kristie. Hopefully, she would be willing to talk to him. The way he saw it, they both needed each other.

Chapter 6

Curtis picked up the strange-looking black phone. He lifted the receiver and then hung it back on its cradle. His father had fallen asleep in his chair and was now snoring loudly. Maybe he should try reaching his mother again. Curtis's father still clutched his beer in his hand, and several empty bottles lay at his feet. Curtis had once asked his father why he needed all that medicine to make him sleep. But his dad had gotten mad at him for asking and yelled.

Curtis missed his mother so much it hurt in the place in his chest where his heart was supposed to be. He missed sleeping in his own bed and hated having to share a lumpy mattress with his father. His father smelled of smoke and the medicine he was constantly drinking. Curtis had already tried calling his mom to come get him. But he had to wait until his father was asleep because he didn't want to get caught.

At first he'd had trouble with the old phone. His

fingers barely fit into the round holes where the numbers were. When he tried dialing, the numbers didn't move. Then he figured out it was easier if he used a pencil to dial. A woman who spoke the strange language his dad called Spanish had answered and screamed at him. Her repeated yelling made him cry. But he'd been afraid to bawl too loudly because his dad might hear and wake up.

One morning his father had left him eating breakfast with the landlady, Senora Gonzales. Pobrecito, her dog, lay at his feet. Curtis had bravely asked how to call the United States, saying that his father wanted him to let his grandmother know just how much fun they were having in Mexico. He figured he'd better say grandmother since Earl had told the old lady his wife was dead.

Senora Gonzales spoke only pidgin English and she had to get her daughter, Esperanza, to help. Esperanza had written down exactly how to call America. Then she'd told him his father would have to pay for the call. Curtis had insisted he'd pay for it himself. He had saved every penny of his allowance and hidden it in his socks.

Tonight looked like a good time to try his mom again. His father was asleep with the television on and most likely would remain so for the night.

On tiptoe, Curtis crept toward the phone, lifted the receiver, and used the pencil to dial. He waited for the connection to be made, listened as the phone rang and the answering machine came on. The sound of his mother's voice made him cry.

Suddenly the phone was knocked out of his hand, and he was grabbed by the back of his T-shirt and flung across the room. When he tried to get up his father stood over him, an angry expression on his face.

"What the hell are you doing?" Earl yelled.

"I was trying to reach Mommy," Curtis sniffed, blinking back the tears that were beginning to form.

"I don't want you touching that blasted phone," his father said, yanking at the cord and pulling it out of the wall. "You understand?"

"But why? Mommy will want to hear about our vacation," Curtis sobbed.

"Your mother doesn't want to hear from you."

"Yes, she does. Mommy loves me. I miss her. She says that I am her special boy."

"Then why isn't your mother here with us?" his father snarled, looking like he wanted to hit him. "Your mommy is too busy for both of us, that's why she gave you to me."

Curtis managed to scramble to his feet. Tears slid down his cheeks as he faced his father. "My mommy didn't give me away. She wouldn't do that."

Earl opened the small refrigerator at the side of the bed, reached in, and took out a beer. "Your mommy doesn't want you or me."

Curtis hurt so badly he felt as if he would throw up. His mommy had promised him that they would never be apart. She'd said they'd be together forever and ever.

"That's not true," he shouted at his father and stamped his foot. "My mommy would never give me away."

"Shut up, you little monster," his father screamed back. "Go wash your face and get into bed."

Curtis didn't want to wash his face or get into bed. He hated his father and hated this ugly room.

He wanted his house, his bike, and his friends. He made up his mind to run away.

When Kristie returned from the grocery store the first thing she noticed was the red light blinking on the answering machine. She set down the groceries on the kitchen counter and pushed the Play button, waiting with the usual trepidation for her messages.

There was the static of a long-distance connection and a muffled voice in the background, but no words she could hear. This wasn't the first time this had happened and Kristie's motherly intuition told her that her son was trying to reach her. Heart slamming against her chest, she looked at her caller ID. The number was blocked. She'd wanted to keep her anguish private and had hoped that Earl would get bored playing father and bring Curtis home. But as time went by she was slowly realizing that finding her son was not going to be a private matter. Much as she hated to do it, it was time to take drastic action. She would need to distribute flyers wherever she could.

Someone had suggested to Kristie that she log on to the Internet and use search engines to find sites that might help her. She realized she should have done this a long time ago but mentally she hadn't been up to it. She'd been in deep denial, hoping that Earl would bring Curtis home. Why would a father want to kidnap his own son? It wasn't as if she'd prevented the boy from seeing his dad.

Kristie had also hoped that experts such as the police and the FBI would already have found Curtis, making any public plea for assistance unnecessary. She'd been wrong.

As Kristie logged on to Google she was amazed by the number of sites that popped up when she used search words like "missing children." She surfed sites with names like North America Missing Children, the Nation Center for Missing and Exploited Children, and then spent a bit longer viewing the information Interpol had to offer. Next she logged on to another site offering support to the loved ones of missing children. This particular parent-advocacy group produced and distributed information nationally.

Kristie became particularly interested in a site called www.beyondmissing.com, which purported to be revolutionary. It allowed registered law enforcement agencies to create and distribute flyers to targeted agencies. It also permitted parents to create and download database information from their desktops.

Kristie's eyes were growing gritty but she was determined to continue to read. Www.beyondmissing.com offered invaluable tips. Helpful hints that she had not followed, such as notifying the local media assignment desks and the nonprofit child-locator services. It also mentioned it was necessary to keep the home phone attended by a living, breathing person, someone the missing child would know. This was definitely worth doing, especially given the number of hang-ups she'd had recently. She'd have to think of someone she could forward her phone calls to.

The phone rang just as Kristie logged on to another site. Sighing loudly, she heaved herself up and immediately felt guilty. What if Curtis was trying to reach her? She forgot about caller ID and snatched up the receiver.

"Hello."

"Hey, girl. Did I catch you at a bad time?" Lizette asked.

Kristie suppressed her disappointment. Just like Lizette to call this late to dish.

"How did it go with Ed?" Kristie asked, knowing that was expected of her.

Lizette groaned. "You don't want to know."

"That bad?"

"Ummm-hmmm."

Kristie's friend didn't sound elated. She felt awful for her. Lizette had headed off all starry-eyed to get ready for her date with Ed Sloan, but now it sounded like things hadn't gone well.

"Did he get fresh?" Kristie prompted, her concern for her friend kicking in.

"No. It was mostly just harmless flirting. But he did tick me off. He kept bringing up your name and implying that you weren't doing everything you could to get Curtis back. I suspect the police department has this crazy notion that you're somehow involved or maybe in cahoots with Earl."

"What!"

"You heard me."

Clutching the remote, Kristie sat down. "Okay, you tell me word for word what Ed Sloan said."

Lizette recited the conversation verbatim and Kristie massaged her aching head. How could anyone think she was a suspect? She loved her child and desperately wanted him back.

She hung up, thinking how unfair life is. All she'd

done was try to follow the judge's mandate and let her child spend time with his father. What had she gotten for that except a slap in the face and her innards wrenched out?

When the phone rang again, Kristie leapt for it. Who could be calling her after eleven? No one who knew her well. This time she glanced at her caller ID and didn't recognize the number but the area code was a Long Island one.

"Hello," Kristie answered wearily.

"Kristie Phillips, please."

It was a male voice, one she didn't recognize.

"This is Kristie. Who's this?"

"Ryan Velox. I'm a broadcaster from the WLIL station. I think you called us the other day."

She was wide-awake now. "What can I do for you, Ryan?"

"I'm working on a story and thought you might help."

"What kind of story are we talking about? And why me?"

"Why not you? You live on Long Island and you have a child that's missing."

Maybe this was the answer to a prayer.

Ryan continued, "My program will feature missing children and focus on the families that are left behind."

Opportunity had come knocking on her door. Should she turn her back on it because of her stupid need for privacy? A little voice in the back of Kristie's head reminded her that all the Web sites had suggested that family members get as much press as they could.

"I'd like to interview you," Ryan Velox insisted. "When are you free?"

"That depends."

"It'll be at your convenience. Your son's been missing going on almost a week. The sooner your story airs, the sooner you're apt to get results."

Ryan Velox seemed to know a lot about her situation. Kristie wondered who'd been running their mouth. She thought about her plans for the week, deciding that tomorrow was out. Her lunch appointment with Zan would set her back, brief as she intended it to be.

"What about later this week?" Kristie countered. "Friday then?"

"Yes, Friday's good but it will have to be after work."

"You'll come to the station?"

"Yes, if you'd like. Just as long as you're not planning on interviewing me live. I'm nervous."

Kristie figured she would speak with Zan tomorrow and see what he thought. She'd need coaching as she didn't want to make things worse or say anything that was totally inappropriate. It was bad enough that the police thought she might be involved in Curtis's abduction. She needed the public's sympathy and needed them on her side.

"May I bring my attorney?" Kristie impulsively asked.

Ryan's audible release of breath filled her ear. "Why would you need an attorney?"

Why indeed? Except that Zan had already demonstrated he was looking out for her, and having him there would make her feel good.

"Because he's a friend," she answered. "If this is

on the up-and-up, there shouldn't be a problem."

"It's on the up-and-up all right. Let me give you my number."

Ryan proceeded to give her the phone number and address of WLIL.

She scribbled it down, deciding that if Zan didn't think it was a good idea, she would call Ryan Velox and cancel.

All that talking had worn Kristie out. She hung up the phone with a throbbing head, shut down her computer, and went to bed. Tomorrow she would get up early and search through what remained of Earl's things. Then she would call the telephone company and the police, and request a tracer put on her phone. She was certain that her son was attempting to reach her but couldn't get through.

Zan had completed his two-mile jog. He now limped back to his house wearily. His caseload had made it impossible to get to the gym as frequently as he liked, and his stress-filled body shouted that it needed exercise.

Using the towel draped around his neck, he swiped at his sweaty face before letting himself into the house. He always made a habit of running along the shore. There was something about sand under his feet and the sound of waves pounding against the rocks that made him relax. Tonight, though his body had taken a beating, his mind refused to relax. He'd thought about Kristie Phillips as he ran and couldn't get her out of his mind.

Kristie's heart-shaped face and huge amber eyes filled his vision. The image made him realize how much he missed having someone special in his life. He'd had his share of flings of course. But as he got older he'd found them to be a waste of time. It didn't seem worth the effort to expend time on a friendship that deep down you knew was going nowhere. That attitude must have been communicated to the women he bedded, because inevitably they grew tired and left him to pursue more obtainable men.

Zan picked up his cell phone from the coffee table where he'd thrown it, glanced at it, and considered not replaying his messages. Habit was hard to break. He noted that Bill Federicks, the detective he'd hired to help Kristie find Curtis, had called.

Although exhausted he should return the man's call. Zan punched the appropriate number and waited for the detective to answer.

"Bill Federicks at your service."

"Bill, this is Zan McManus," Zan said. "What have you got for me?"

"Not much. But I did speak to a woman who thinks that she saw Leone and his son at the airport."

"Did she see them get on a plane?"

"No. She works at the terminal at one of those overpriced fast food chains. Someone matching Leone's description bought a hot dog for his son that Sunday night. She remembers them because the little boy kept telling his father that he hated hot dogs, but the man kept telling him to shut up and eat it, that's all he would get."

Zan ran a hand across his shaved head. "Once Ms. Phillips supplies us with a photograph of her ex you might try showing the woman that. You will be meeting with her again?"

"I plan to. She likes to talk and, uh, I think she likes me."

"Then work that angle. What about the passenger lists?"

"I've got a buddy working in reservations at American who owes me a favor."

"Good. How about Earl Leone's parents? Have you called them?"

Bill cleared his throat. "I called pretending to be a solicitor and they hung up on me."

"Try the straightforward approach," Zan suggested, "and get back to me."

Zan hung up with the detective and headed for the shower. But even a lukewarm shower did nothing to get Kristie Phillips out of his head. He couldn't wait to see her tomorrow.

Chapter 7

The first thing Lizette noticed when she stepped out of her Volkswagen Bug was the Blazer parked in front of the school, and illegally at that.

She had ten minutes to make it to class and she practically raced across the parking lot. She'd stop in the bathroom first, touch up her makeup, and make sure she wasn't too windblown.

"Hey, Lizette, wait up," a deep male voice growled behind her.

What was Ed Sloan doing here?

Lizette turned, her eyes almost popping out of her head when he stepped from the vehicle and loped to her side. Today he was much more casually attired in a sweatsuit and sneakers. But even so the man was as sexy as any man could get.

Ed's large hand circled her elbow, halting her progress. Lizette's heart leapt into her mouth and her entire body tingled. She wished that he would take his hand off her. She had young minds to develop, and the thoughts that his long, lean frame evoked were not the kind a teacher should have.

"I'm here to apologize and to convince you to have lunch with me," Ed said.

"I don't eat lunch," Lizette answered, batting her eyelashes at him and telling a bald-faced lie.

"Make an exception."

Boy, he was pushy. She glanced at the watch on the arm he was still holding. "I have to go or I'll be late."

"Not until you promise to go out with me again."

"Call me," she said, wrenching her arm free. "I'll check my schedule and see if I have time."

She knew it was a snooty response but Ed deserved it. He was probably used to women throwing themselves at his feet. The truth was that she was still miffed at him for what he'd said about Kristie.

Footsteps behind her indicated that he'd followed her to the door. Lizette glanced over her shoulder to find him right there.

"Give a guy a break. How about a kiss good-bye?" Ed asked.

Lizette shot him a look that clearly said he was out of his mind. "This is where I work," she reminded him.

"So?"

"So, as the saying goes, I don't eat and you know what in the same place."

Ed's shoulders shook. He threw his head back and roared. "You're something else, Lizette Stokes."

"The same could be said of you." She eased the door open and wiggled her fingers at him. "I'll wait for your call."

"Count on it."

Lizette practically slammed the door in his face. He was cocky and full of himself but she liked him.

A hectic morning followed. Soon it was time for lunch. As Lizette stepped out of her classroom Kristie raced by.

"Hey, what's the hurry?" Lizette asked, scurrying to catch up with her friend.

"Zan's waiting in the parking lot."

"Oh? T. Zan McManus paying a house call to one of his clients. How come?"

"We need to go over some details and I've got to give him a photo of Earl and information about some of the people he might know." Kristie waved a manila envelope.

"This sounds more like a date than business to me," Lizette said dryly.

Kristie arched an eyebrow. "Now what would Zan McManus see in me?"

"Plenty." She eyed her friend, always amazed at how unassuming she was.

Kristie was the kind of woman that men gravitated to immediately. Largely because she was not aware of the effect she had on them. She was beautiful and didn't know it, with the kind of body that stopped traffic. Plus she had a vulnerability to her that made men feel like men.

"I've got to go," Kristie said, attempting to rush by. "I've got forty minutes for lunch. I know you do too."

"Okay, you'll give me the lowdown later."

"Yes."

Outside, Kristie spotted Zan's silver Lexus. The windows were down and he slouched in the driver's seat, face tilted to the sun. Zan spotted her, shrugged out of his jacket, and got out of the car carrying a wicker basket. He was wearing dark glasses and looked both mysterious and formidable.

"Sorry," Kristie said. "One of my kids kept asking questions. It was hard to get away."

Zan placed a hand on her shoulder. "Sounds like you're a very caring teacher, Kristie Phillips."

"I try."

"Where should we have lunch? Pick some place quiet."

Kristie suggested the park across the street.

"I don't have a lot of time," she reminded him as they headed toward the picnic tables where a handful of people sat.

"This shouldn't take long."

They sat at a table away from the few people enjoying the sun. Zan began unpacking the picnic basket and Kristie handed him her envelope.

"That's the best I could do. The photo's not very good but should give you at least an idea of what my ex looks like. I did find quite a few pictures of Curtis and I've added them in. Additionally, I found an old address and phone book of Earl's that might be useful to us."

Zan stopped his unpacking and patted Kristie's hand.

"You did well on short notice," he said, handing her a baguette crammed with luncheon meats, lettuce, and tomatoes. "Tell me you're not on a diet."

"Never on a diet," Kristie admitted.

"Then you're the rare one." He sank his teeth into a whole-wheat sandwich filled with what looked like turkey and pushed the container with pickles in her direction.

"Dill," he said though she hadn't asked. Pointing to the other containers, he explained, "There's potato salad, coleslaw, and I even got soup."

"Where did this all come from?" Kristie inquired, not able to picture the man in his starched white shirt performing even the simplest of domestic duties.

"Village deli," he confirmed. "I'm a mess in the kitchen. I have a very close and intimate relationship with my neighborhood grocer. We need each other."

Kristie giggled. Zan McManus was funny and wasn't as intimidating as he'd initially appeared. Yes, he looked out of place in business attire, sitting on a picnic bench, long legs splayed, biting hungrily into a sandwich. But at the same time he looked more human.

"You should do that more often," he said, suddenly growing serious.

"Do what more often?"

"Smile."

"There hasn't been much to smile about lately," she reminded him and herself.

Zan slid a bottle of spring water toward her. "I know that, hon. But if I have anything to do with it, that will change."

Kristie didn't want to misunderstand him. She assumed that he was simply talking about finding Curtis. Zan probably called everyone "hon," though it seemed a casual and intimate term for a lawyer to be using.

She changed the subject abruptly. "Ever heard of Ryan Velox?"

"The name sounds familiar."

"He's a cable newscaster."

"Oh, yes, of course."

"He called last night and wanted to interview me."

Zan stopped chewing. "Why?"

"Well, that's the thing, he says he's working on a story about missing children and the families left behind."

"What did you say to him? Did you agree?"

Kristie wished she could see Zan's eyes and their expression, but he still wore his dark glasses. She could only go by his tone, a tone that was carefully guarded.

"I said I'd do it if he would allow my attorney to accompany me."

"Good girl," Zan said, surprising her by whipping off his glasses and moving over to sit beside her. "Then what did he say?"

God, she wished he hadn't done that, gotten close to her. The scent of a masculine cologne drifted over and she could barely breathe. Her heart beat erratically as Zan's thigh pressed against her leg. She assumed that had happened accidentally. But when he looked at her she forgot why she was here. Better to concentrate on the sandwich that now lodged in her throat and not on the man who'd made it difficult to swallow.

When she dared speak, Kristie said, "Ryan Velox didn't seem exactly enthused by the idea of you accompanying me. He wanted to know why I needed my attorney."

"And you told him?"

Zan's eyes never left Kristie's face. She felt flushed under his intense scrutiny.

"I told him you were my attorney and friend."

"Am I your friend?" Zan asked, his gray eyes sweeping her face.

Talk about boxing her in. "Yes, of course, unless you'd prefer not to be."

"What day and time is this interview?" Zan asked, changing the subject. He removed a pocket organizer from his pants pocket and began pushing buttons.

"Friday after work."

"Make it around seven. I'll need time to wrap up, get to Baldwin, then drive to Massapequa. That is where the station is?"

Kristie nodded. "You're picking me up at my house?" she asked, surprised that he would.

"Is that a problem?"

"No, no problem."

But it was. It would mean that she'd be forced to ask him in and he'd see how simply she lived. Maybe that wasn't such a bad thing. It might help to keep her legal fees reasonable.

"Good, then it's all set. I'll come by your place at six-thirty P.M," Zan said.

He finished the last of his sandwich, laid fruit and cheese out on a paper plate, and using a pocket-knife began paring an apple. He offered a wedge of both cheese and apple to Kristie.

"No, thanks. My forty minutes are almost up," she said, and began to help him tidy up.

"A pity." He made short work of the apple and cheese. "Listen, before I forget. Bill, the detective we retained, found a woman at the airport who thinks she saw Earl and Curtis. The photo you gave me will help determine if what she says is true."

Kristie was afraid to hope. While she didn't know where her son was, she was confident he was alive. Earl, as irresponsible as he might be, loved his boy, and would not harm him; that in and of itself was comforting. It was small consolation but the only thing she had left.

She crossed the street, returning to the school, Zan's hand on the small of her back. His touch burned a hole through the starched cotton shirt she'd paired with hip-hugging slacks. He surprised her by walking her to the Learning Center's front door.

"Thanks for having lunch with me," Zan said. "We should do this more often, maybe once a week."

"Why?" Her puzzlement reflected in her voice, making her sound ungracious. She tried to recover. "It's just I know you're busy and the ride from Garden City to Merrick isn't exactly short."

Zan cleared his throat. "I'm never too busy for you. I mean for a client. I'll be in touch, Kristie. Meanwhile, you stay safe."

Turning on his heel, he left her.

Kristie stared for a long time at his broad back, liking the way he carried himself, as if the world were his, and he would allow nothing and no one to stand in his way.

She could only hope that the same carried over to the way he did business. It was time to get aggressive and get Curtis back.

"I still can't get that little boy out of my mind," Jude Martin said as she, her husband, and her son waited to board the plane that would take them to the United States. "There was something about his father I didn't like."

"You worry too much," her husband, Henry, said, throwing an arm around his son, Kevin. "The man was harried and didn't exercise good judgment, that's all."

"Yes, I suppose, but he was disheveled looking. He borrowed money from you to pay the cab. Money that you still haven't gotten back."

"I'm not going to lose any sleep over thirty-five bucks," Henry said, yawning and rolling his eyes. "We had a great vacation, but it's time to go home."

"True. I can't wait to sleep in my own bed."

"Kevin, get back here," Jude yelled as her son made a beeline for a store selling clowns and piñatas. She seldom permitted him out of her sight. He was six years old, and impressionable. One couldn't be too careful these days. She'd heard all the stories about children being abducted.

"We're preboarding Flight 597 to JFK Airport. Those with small children or requiring special assistance may now board," an airline employee announced.

Jude looked for Kevin. He'd started up a conversation with what looked to be a male student who was examining the store's merchandise carefully.

"Kevin," Jude yelled again. "Get over here. It's time to go home."

"Coming, Mommy," Kevin, said shuffling his feet and looking like the last thing he wanted to do was get on a plane. The student followed him out and they began an animated conversation.

"Go get your son," Jude ordered Henry. "Get a good hold on his hand. The last thing we need is for him to disappear."

Henry, used to obeying his wife for the sake of keeping peace, loped off. He returned with Kevin just as the airline employee announced, "All remaining passengers on Flight 597 may now board."

Jude at his side, they followed a stream of passengers onto the plane.

Chapter 8

"Nervous?" Zan asked, helping Kristie from the passenger seat of his car. Her hand was ice-cold and he gave it a little squeeze. It surprised him that he liked playing the role of protector and coach to a woman who obviously needed his help.

Zan ignored the voice at the back of his mind that said, *Kristie Phillips is the type of woman you love to hate.* She reminded him of his birth mother who had refused to take a more aggressive role in finding him. As a result, she'd ended up losing him for twenty-something years.

"I am nervous," Kristie admitted, bringing Zan back to earth. "What if Ryan Velox starts badgering me? What if he makes me out to be a bad parent?"

"Then he'll have me to answer to," Zan said fiercely.

He locked the car doors. It was exactly five minutes to seven and the parking lot of WLIL was almost empty. He and Kristie had spent the last twenty minutes prepping for this interview with Ryan Velox.

Zan had suggested to Kristie that she be open and honest. She needed the public on her side. It would not serve her well to be defensive if Ryan's questions became overly personal or he attempted to pry. It also would not be in Kristie's best interest if Zan appeared on the air with her. It might look like she had something to hide. His role would be one of moral support and his presence would put Ryan Velox on notice that if he boxed his client into a corner he'd have to answer to him.

And answer to him Velox would. Kristie had become very dear to Zan in a relatively short period of time. He'd cautioned himself over and over again not to let his attraction get in the way of business. She was not what he was looking for or what he had in mind. He did not want a wife with a ready-made family, nor did he want a woman without the proverbial pot to pee in. What he wanted was a strong woman who would be his equal.

Zan wasn't necessarily looking for a wealthy woman. In fact he wasn't currently looking for a woman at all. However, when he selected a wife he wanted one that brought something to the table. That way he could be sure she hadn't picked him because he had a successful law practice. Not that he thought Kristie was an opportunist, far from it. He just didn't want a woman totally dependent on him, like his mother had been on his father.

"Ready?" he asked, offering Kristie his arm.

"As ready as I ever will be."

They entered a revolving door, walked through the lobby, and took the elevator up to the fifth floor.

Ryan Velox, a very handsome man who appeared stuck on himself, met them in the reception room.

COME BACK TO ME

Introductions were made and then Kristie was whisked into an inner room. She darted a glance over her shoulder and Zan gave her the thumbs-up sign, silently communicating that he was there for her. A half hour later she emerged, looking drained and as if she'd been put through the ringer.

"How did it go?" Zan asked when they were again seated in the Lexus.

"I'm not sure."

"What types of questions did Velox ask you?"

"Nothing too intrusive. He wanted to know how long Curtis has been gone and why I waited until now to make a public plea. He also wanted to know what steps I've taken to get him back. Did I distribute flyers, that kind of thing. What type of relationship did I have with my ex?"

"Speaking of flyers, I think that's a good idea to get some out. In fact that's something we should have done already. How did you respond to Velox?"

"I answered as honestly as I could," Kristie said, laying her head back against the seat and closing her eyes. "I told Ryan I guarded my privacy fiercely and that up until now I'd relied on word of mouth."

Zan didn't know what made him do it but he leaned across and squeezed her thigh. "This calls for a drink. You look like you could use one."

Kristie opened her eyes. "Yes, I think I could."

"We'll make a stop and have a quick one."

Zan resisted the urge to wrap her in his arms and shield her from all that was unpleasant. He detoured to a tiny café he knew of in nearby Wantagh. The owner was from the islands and the décor had a definite Caribbean flavor to it. It was a step up from the usual watering hole and he was certain Kristie would enjoy it.

Zan pulled into a parking lot with a neon sign that read THE ISLAND INN. Only a few cars were parked and he easily found a space.

The inside was dimly lit. They were seated upstairs under a faux coconut tree. Zan ordered Rum-Runners for them.

"Feel better?" he asked after Kristie took her first sip.

"Nothing will make me feel better until I have my son back," she said quietly.

"I'm doing everything in my power to make that possible," he said, taking her hand.

"I know you are."

Fingers linked, he stared into her eyes, hoping that he could imbue his strength into her. Kristie Phillips was beginning to get under his skin and prudence dictated he maintain a professional distance.

"Tell me about yourself?" Zan asked.

"There's not that much to tell."

She ran a cinnamon hand through cropped curls and recited, "I'm thirty years old, but I think you already know that. I married Earl when I was twenty-two and fresh out of college."

"What do you do with your free time?"

"Free time? I haven't had much of that."

"You must do something on weekends when you're off."

"When my son was with me I'd take him to the park or to a soccer game."

"And now that he isn't, what are you doing to eliminate stress?" He squeezed her hand. It felt like parchment in his, as if it would crack.

"I read," she said, blinking in response to his question. "Sometimes I rollerblade. And I visit my sister in New Jersey."

"So basically you're putting one foot in front of the other."

She chuckled grimly. "I've been a mother and wife for most of my adult years. My child was my whole existence."

Kristie's life was far different from Zan's. His was filled with consultations and trials. The few spare moments he had he devoted to exercise, and weather permitting, he went out on his boat.

Impulsively Zan asked, "What are you doing this weekend?"

Kristie looked at him guardedly. "I'm catching up on chores. If I have time I'll visit my sister, or if Lizette's available, we'll go to a movie."

"Any chance I can persuade you to come out and visit me?"

Kristie stared at him as if he had two heads. Zan didn't know why he'd issued the invitation. He'd definitely crossed the line. Not good.

"I don't know," Kristie answered, tugging her hand away and folding it primly in her lap. "You're my attorney. I wouldn't feel right coming to your home."

"I just came to yours," Zan pointed out. He finished his drink and signaled the waiter for the check.

"That's different." Kristie picked up her purse and waited for Zan to settle the bill.

"What's different about it? By this weekend I should have more information for you." He placed his hand on her elbow and steered her down the winding staircase.

Kristie gave him a wide-eyed amber look and let him continue to guide her.

She didn't know it yet but Zan didn't plan on taking no for an answer.

The buzzer at the front door rang.

Lizette, who'd been keeping an eye on her shrimp scampi dinner, raced from the kitchen and pressed an eye to the peephole. She saw a broad chest but no face to go with it.

"Who is it?" she called.

"Lizette, it's Ed."

Lizette took a deep breath and debated whether to let him in.

"What are you doing here?" she asked.

"Some way to greet your man."

Cocky and full of himself, but that was Ed.

"I have no man," Lizette yelled back.

"Better open up quickly or the entire floor's going to hear what I have to say to that."

Ed's voice was syrupy sweet, challenging.

"You wouldn't dare."

"Try me."

Lizette yanked the front door open. Ed towered above her, a six-foot-four Adonis with a killer smile. He sauntered in.

Lizette stared at him openmouthed as he made himself comfortable on her sectional couch.

"Come sit with me," he said, patting the place beside him.

The nerve.

Soft jazz played on the stereo and a delicious aroma wafted in from the kitchen. She needed to get back to her shrimp scampi before it was ruined.

"Something smells wonderful," Ed said, legs splayed, nose sniffing the air appreciatively.

"*My* dinner," she said curtly, making a beeline for the kitchen.

Ed followed, coming up behind her. Lizette swung around and rammed into his slab of a chest. Tight jeans molded to powerful legs and a cotton long-sleeved T-shirt barely contained his muscles.

"Easy," Ed said, grabbing her by the shoulders. His powerful male scent made her senses go reeling.

"Do you want a beer?" Lizette asked, thinking quickly how best to get away from him.

"Yeah, I could use a cold brew."

Lizette handed Ed a Bud. He gulped down the liquid in several quick swallows and ambled to the stove.

"You've got enough there for two," he said pointedly.

"I take it you're inviting yourself to dinner?"

"No point in eating alone," he said, reaching into the overhead cabinets and removing two plates.

She couldn't believe the gall he had.

"Since you've invited yourself, make yourself useful and take the dishes into the living room. We'll eat at the coffee table," she said.

Ed sat on a pillow on the floor while she served salad and shrimp scampi. By the end of the meal he was on his third beer. Lizette sipped wine and thought how pushy he was. Pushy but cute. No point in being annoyed with him.

"Come over here," Ed said, after she'd cleaned up. He patted a spot on the sofa next to him.

Lizette sat stiffly. Ed draped a long arm around her shoulders and with his nose, nuzzled her neck.

"I may be in love," Ed said, giving her an open-mouthed kiss while attempting to work her shirt out of her pants.

Lizette slid away from him, slapping at his roaming hands. "You're moving too fast for me."

He was a player all right. Better keep that in mind or she would get hurt.

"Where's your buddy tonight?" Ed asked, his hands caressing her arms.

"Which buddy?"

"There's only one I know of."

"Kristie?"

"Uh-huh."

She debated whether to tell him that Kristie was being interviewed. Maybe that would convince him that her friend was actively attempting to find her child.

"Kristie's at an interview with Ryan Velox of WLIL."

"Took her long enough to go public."

"So you approve?"

"Why wouldn't I? The more publicity her case gets the easier my job becomes. If people are aware that a child's been abducted they'll call in leads. If Curtis Leone's face is shown on the news, the odds of finding him improve."

Lizette tapped Ed's almost empty beer bottle. "Good point. You want another beer?"

"Sure, I'll have another."

"You'll be okay to drive?"

Ed laughed. His blue eyes roamed around the room. "I don't plan on leaving."

He was clearly sober and hadn't missed a beat or detail of her apartment. Earlier he'd wandered around the living room touching knickknacks and commenting.

Lizette poured another glass of wine and brought back the beer Ed requested.

"Where's your bedroom?" he asked, getting up.

She gave him her vapid look and pretended to be puzzled. "Why would my bedroom interest you?"

"Because it usually reflects the owner's personality. Show me the real Lizette Stokes," Ed said, grabbing her hand and pulling her up against him. He stuck his tongue in her ear. When she refused to react he continued, "If you don't show me I'll find it on my own."

Ed started down the hallway, tugging her along. He was assertive and bossy but she did like him. He opened the closed door, entered her bedroom, and surveyed the decor. A queen-sized bed was shrouded in cream-colored gauze. The spread was a quilt of burgundy and champagne velvet squares. Hardwood floors held scatter rugs designed to complement the Chinese-red walls she'd painted herself. A bookshelf housed books, ceramic urns, and dried flowers and on a rocking chair her precious collection of china dolls stared through marble eyes. The scent of potpourri and vanilla candles permeated the air.

"Well, whaddya know?" Ed said, grinning. "My girl's romantic. She's got style."

"Your girl?"

"My girl," he said, looping his arms around her neck and drawing her close.

He pushed her shirt up almost to her neck and his cool hands kneaded her flesh. Lizette inhaled

Ed's cologne and forgot about barely knowing him and not really trusting him. His face was already buried between her breasts.

"What are you doing?" she managed as his tongue traced a warm path between her cleavage.

"Loving you. Is that a problem?"

She wanted to say it was, but the words stuck in her throat. Ed's hands on her body felt good. Very good.

"I hardly know you," she protested.

"What is there to know? I'm good looking, gainfully employed, and have no communicable diseases. I've already told you, you're my girl."

"But this is the third time we've seen each other."

"The third time's a charm," Ed said, tickling her sides and making her laugh. "We're feeling each other. Let's go with the flow."

"Pretty sure of yourself, aren't you?"

"I know what I want," Ed said, cupping her buttocks and pressing her up against the long, hard length of him. "Ed Junior knows what he wants too."

Lizette's defenses collapsed and her body went on fire. Ed's teeth nibbled at her earlobe. His hands stroked her bare midriff and crept upward to cover her breasts. He lodged a leg between hers and she sat down on it, riding that leg until she was engorged and pulsating.

"Oh, God," Lizette cried, "I do want you."

"Now you're talking, babe," Ed said, easing her toward the bed before stopping to tug off his shirt and loosen his belt. "Get naked, will ya?"

The order was succinct and to the point. Too late to play coy. She wanted him as badly as he wanted her. Lizette stripped off her clothing.

Ed let out a piercing wolf whistle. "Mama, mia. You've got some body, babe."

Lizette was suddenly conscious of her wide hips and of her belly that would never be flat and had a tendency to dimple.

One of Ed's hands cupped her butt, the other angled her chin up. She slid a hand down the back of his jeans and discovered he wore no underwear. Ed shifted away, unzipped his pants, and stepped out of them. He turned, offering himself up.

His hand pressed her head down and Lizette's knees buckled. She took him into her mouth, and found his hot spot. Ed's ecstatic grunting got louder. He bucked against her.

"Keep going," he groaned when Lizette paused for breath. All she could concentrate on was keeping Ed Junior stationary in her mouth while she pleasured him.

Grasping her hair, Ed signaled enough. Lizette got to her feet and Ed steered her toward the bed.

"Did you bring protection?" she had the presence of mind to ask.

"I never leave home without a condom."

He really was quite the man-about-town.

Lizette lay on her back while Ed retrieved his wallet from his pants. He brought a foil package back with him.

"Help me get this on," he ordered, handing her the packet.

Lizette sheathed him and he climbed on top of her. Using one hand he captured both arms and held them high above her head. The other went to work, stroking, probing, and loving her most intimate places. Ed had a knee between her thighs and she squirmed before settling into him.

Warning bells exploded in Lizette's head. If Ed didn't enter her soon she would find release with or without him. That thought must have been silently communicated, because he drove into her. She soon resided in a place where she'd never been before, where there were no worries, just a lot of pleasure.

She had a vague remembrance of where she was but clearly recalled whom she was with. She bit the sides of Ed's neck and her nails raked his back. She captured him between her legs and held him still. He rammed into her again, this time sending her soaring over the top.

Lizette screamed his name.

Ed held her by the hips and released his seed inside her.

Lizette thought she'd just about died.

Chapter 9

Curtis hated this country called Mexico and hated the little village where he now lived. He hated its funny name, Isle de something he couldn't pronounce. His father told him the word meant artists. He disliked being left alone in the boardinghouse with only Pobrecito and Senora Gonzalez for company while his father went off.

Today he planned on doing something about it. He wanted to go home. But he couldn't even call his mother to tell her that. His dad had broken the cord on the old black phone when he'd pulled it out of the wall. Mrs. Gonzalez was afraid to let him use her phone because his dad had told her that if she did, he would pack up and leave. She needed the money his dad paid her. The old lady was scared to death that she would have to answer to his father if Curtis even tried calling the United States. He'd said Curtis's grandmother didn't want to hear from him.

Senora Gonzalez had nodded and mumbled, *"Sí, senor. Sí, sí. Comprendo."*

And she did understand.

So the only thing left to do was to run away. Curtis had thought about it carefully. He would have to get a ride to the airport, but first he would have to call his mother so that she could pick him up. Maybe that nice Mr. Santiago would help.

Curtis was prepared for the trip. He'd started stealing dollar bills from his dad's wallet whenever he drank too much medicine and fell asleep in the chair. The dollars along with the allowance Curtis had kept hidden from his father should be enough. He'd not taken any pesos because he didn't understand how to use them.

He slid a hand into the socks he kept balled up and slowly began counting out bills. There was a total of fifteen dollars, enough to buy a phone card at Mr. Santiago's shop and have some left over, he hoped. The shopkeeper spoke a little English and when Curtis's dad was not looking he'd give him free candy. He'd say in his funny voice, "Here, sweetie for you. You try, no?"

Curtis always tried the chewy candy and said it was good. He always thanked Mr. Santiago, who would then pat his head. His dad usually went behind the store, returning all happy, his clothes smelling of smoke.

"Hey, Pobrecito, you want to go home with me?" Curtis asked, stroking the dog's wiry fur. The mutt's ribs stuck out at odd angles and his teeth were crooked.

The dog looked at Curtis adoringly and licked his hand.

"I'll find a way to bring you home with me," Curtis promised, glancing around to see if Senora Gonzalez was still stirring her pot. She was making chicken and rice and it smelled up the whole house. Her daughter, Esperanza, was at work and returned home complaining about her feet every evening. She waited tables at a café in another town.

Senora Gonzalez was nowhere to be found. She was probably in the little garden out back, picking peas that she would shell later. Curtis crept toward the back door and heard the rustle of leaves as Senora Gonzalez picked her peas. She was speaking to herself in the funny language he didn't understand. Curtis tiptoed back, took off his belt, and looped it into the metal ring of Pobrecito's collar.

"You be quiet now," he warned the dog, tugging gently on the makeshift leash and heading out the front door.

Senora Gonzalez called to him in Spanglish, "Attencion. Curtis. You watch television."

Curtis began speaking quickly, knowing that she would not understand. "Yes, I'm watching television in my room. Pobrecito's sitting with me."

With that he was out the door and running down the street, the dog happily beside him. Today he didn't have time to visit with the artists and look wishfully at the clowns and colorful paintings they sold. He had to get to the store, buy a phone card, and make his call before his dad or Senora Gonzalez realized he was gone.

"Hey, hey," one of the men selling ice cones called to Curtis as he raced by. The man held up a dripping snow cone and waved at him to come over.

Curtis shook his head and continued on his way.

He didn't stop running until he reached Mr. Santiago's shop and even then he raced around the back to make sure his father was not in the alleyway. If he ran into his dad he'd already thought up a good story. Curtis would tell him that he was lonely and had come looking for him. He knew he risked a beating but it was a chance he was willing to take. He wanted to go home.

Curtis entered the store and quickly walked up to the counter.

"Buenos dias," Mr. Santiago said. "You come alone?"

Curtis pointed to Pobrecito. "My dog came with me."

"Bueno." Mr. Santiago smiled. He didn't seem to mind having Pobrecito in his store.

Pobrecito let out a little bark and wagged his tail. He liked Mr. Santiago.

"You want candy?" the store owner asked, holding out a plate with a sticky substance on it that was cut into squares.

Curtis nodded, took a piece, and offered some to Pobrecito. The dog went wild and began yapping for more.

"Shush," Curtis said, then turned to the shopkeeper. "Can I buy a phone card, please?" He took the money out of his pocket and slapped it down on the counter. "Is this enough?"

Mr. Santiago took the cash and began counting in the strange language that was Spanish.

"Where you calling?" he asked.

"America. My mother."

"Didn't your father say your mother was—" He bent over, reached into a glass case, and took out a card. "This cost ten dollars. You wouldn't be able to talk for long but it should get you through."

The card had a lizard with a pink tongue on it. Mr. Santiago pointed to the phones at the back of the store. "Use those."

Curtis took Pobrecito with him and entered a phone booth. He tried reading the tiny lettering on the card and decided he needed help. He returned to the store owner but had to wait in line.

Several customers had entered the store and Curtis made sure that none of them were his father. He waited until Mr. Santiago had finished selling newspapers and postcards and told him he didn't know what to do. Mr. Santiago took the phone card, picked up his own receiver, and asked for the number he wanted to call.

Curtis, realizing he needed to move quickly, let Mr. Santiago punch in the numbers. He told Curtis to come behind the counter and handed him the phone. It rang and rang and finally the answering machine picked up.

"Mommy, are you there?" Curtis asked, holding his breath, hoping that she was. Sometimes his mommy liked to hear the person's voice before picking up.

"I want to come home. I hate it here," Curtis wailed, knowing that he sounded like a baby. "This artist island isn't fun. I miss you and Daddy's mean. I'm going to find a plane to come home."

Pobrecito began to yelp and Curtis quickly hung up the receiver. He glanced behind him to see who'd entered the store. It was time to go before the adults noticed that he was alone and began to ask questions.

On his way out the door he waved to Mr. Santiago. The shopkeeper flashed a bright smile and said, "Come back and visit me soon, you hear? Bring your dog with you."

Curtis stood on the sidewalk looking up and down the road. He decided that maybe walking along the main street wasn't such a good idea. What if he ran into his father? He turned down a side street and saw the big buses parked. He began walking toward a building that he thought might be where they left from. He wasn't sure that a bus driver would allow him to bring Pobrecito on board but it was worth asking. He needed to get to an airport as soon as he could.

Curtis entered a dirty building where several people carrying shopping bags of food talked to each other and waited. He couldn't read the signs because he didn't understand the language, so he sat on a bench swinging his legs. Pobrecito sat on the floor beside him. A man came toward them and took the seat next to Curtis. He began speaking in the language Curtis did not understand.

Pobrecito growled.

Curtis looked at the man and tried to explain that he didn't know what he was saying.

"You speak English," the man said, smiling. His teeth were yellow and reminded Curtis of the fox in the story his mother once read him.

"Yes, I speak English."

Pobrecito growled again. He didn't like the man.

"Hush," Curtis said, not wanting all these people to notice that he was alone except for the dog.

"Where you going to?" the yellow-teeth man asked, reaching over to poke Pobrecito with the toe of his sneakers that had a hole in them.

The dog bared his teeth and snapped at the man's ankles. He quickly drew his foot back.

"Nasty *perro*."

"No, he's not," Curtis said, although he wasn't certain what *perro* meant. But the way the man said it didn't sound good. If Pobrecito didn't like the man, he didn't either. "I'm meeting my dad at the airport."

"And taking that dog with you?"

"Yes." Curtis wished the man would go away and leave him alone.

Pobrecito, guessing he was being talked about, bared his teeth and Curtis jerked on the belt he was holding. Pobrecito looked like he wanted to bite the man. Curtis thought quickly. Maybe he should get up and move away.

"Nice talking to you," he said, jumping up and waving to the man.

"Wait. I'll take you where you want to go."

The man had taken car keys from his pocket and he jingled them at Curtis.

"I have a ride," Curtis said, racing for the door, Pobrecito galloping beside him.

He looked over his shoulder to see if the man was following but he was nowhere in sight. To be sure, Curtis kept up his speed for several blocks. Pobrecito's tongue hung out of his head. He was thirsty.

Curtis spotted a standpipe on the side of the road. He struggled with the faucet and yellow water dripped out. Pobrecito greedily lapped up the water that fell into a gutter below.

It was now midafternoon and Curtis decided he should ask someone how to get to the airport before it got too late. He approached a small restaurant where waiters in black jackets were setting up tables.

One of the waiters spotting Pobrecito began screaming and pointing. "No, no, no. No *perro aqui.*"

Curtis realized he didn't want a dog in the building. Curtis tied Pobrecito to a post on the sidewalk and entered the restaurant.

"Please, do you speak English?" he asked a waiter. His mother had taught him that saying please was good.

"No *inglés,*" the same screaming waiter said, looking at him through narrow eyes.

Another man looked up and jerked his thumb in the direction of a back room. He screamed, "Maria! *Venga aqui.*"

The woman called Maria, who was skinny and blond, came out and glared at them. She smiled at Curtis.

"Hi, kid, what you doing here?"

She sounded American. Safe.

"My dad's down the street waiting for me," Curtis lied. "He wanted me to ask you how to get to the airport. We can't take a taxi because we don't have the money."

Maria made a noise with her mouth. It sounded like water boiling. She said something to the waiters in Spanish. They all seemed to say the same thing, something that sounded like "autobus."

"The bus is your best bet," Maria repeated, squatting down to look Curtis in the eye. "Shouldn't cost you more than a few dollars. Half price for you since you're under twelve." She reached into her pocket and pressed a five-dollar bill into his hand. "If you want you can walk over to the Sheraton. Their courtesy bus leaves every half hour."

"Does courtesy mean that it's free?" Curtis asked.

Maria nodded. "Yeah, just pretend you're one of the hotel guests and hop on board."

Curtis hoped that the free bus would let him take Pobrecito on board. If not he didn't know what he would do. The five dollars Maria had given him helped but he was afraid to return to the bus station because he didn't want to run into the man who'd sat down next to him.

Curtis thanked the blond woman and raced from the restaurant. Outside he looked around for Pobrecito but the dog was nowhere to be found. He ran up and down the street, calling, "Pobrecito, Pobrecito." He began to feel sick. He'd lost Senora Gonzalez's dog.

Adults tried stopping him, speaking to him in the strange language he didn't understand. He was tired and hungry and he was upset because his only friend was gone. Curtis sat on the curb, put his head in his hands, and cried.

First he'd lost his mother, now he'd lost Pobrecito. He wanted to die.

Ryan Velox heard the slow countdown through the earpiece. In exactly two minutes he would be on the air. Ryan was excited. The station had hyped this broadcast about missing children and their families to the max. Now it was up to him to make a good showing. The program would be aired in three segments. Ryan planned on tugging at the emotional heartstrings and getting his audience hooked.

He patted his already perfect hair, helmeted into perfection with mousse, and peered into the monitor. He flashed a seductive smile. Looks were everything in this media business where youth, vitality, and blondness reigned. Ryan was currently the flavor of the month and he meant to keep it that way. He would do any- and everything in his power to stay at the top of his game.

The production assistant gave him the signal. Ryan smiled into the camera, pretending that he was making love to the woman of his dreams. And he was. Broadcasting had seduced him at an early age and his audiences were the voyeurs he allowed into his bedroom.

Women were naturally drawn to programs like his. Tonight, 95 percent of his audience would be female. Ryan would bring them to the brink of orgasm with his movie star looks and melodious tongue. Keeping that in mind, he gave the camera his serious blue-eyed stare. Lips that made even the most frigid woman respond began speaking.

"Good evening, this is your newscaster Ryan Velox of *Long Island Live* with tonight's special presentation. This is the first segment of a three-part broadcast: 'Do you know where your children are?'"

Ryan held the camera's gaze and hoped the cameramen were astute enough to get a close-up shot of his eyes and the moisture he'd forced into them.

He continued, "Thousands of children disappear every year, some never to be seen or heard from again. These children come from all walks of life. Some are affluent, others are the product of a working-class environment. Many are runaways and others are kidnapped by strangers. Some have even been abducted by parents. Long Island, please pay close attention as we show you some of our missing children."

The faces of several missing children flashed on the screen. Ryan grabbed for his glass and gulped down water. When the camera panned back to him he recited the last known national statistics of missing children.

"In the last several years the media have been quick to cover these stories," Ryan said, "but what about the families left behind? How do they cope? How do they continue to live?

"There are many children missing in our own backyards. Families are forced to go through the business of day-to-day living, trying their best to cope. I interviewed three Long Island families whose lives will never be the same. They have all experienced losses. We need your involvement to make them families again."

Close-ups of Kristie Phillips, Herb Sapperstein, and a Latin woman, Rosa Mendoza, flashed on the screen along with photos of their missing children. Ryan had strategically chosen families that were Caucasian, Latino, and African-American. His goal was to reach every ethnic mix and tug on the emotional heartstrings of each of his viewers.

"If you have seen or come into contact with one of these children, pick up your phones and call the toll-free number," Ryan urged, his blue-eyed gaze sweeping the camera. "Long Island, please help these children to come home."

He repeated the number running simultaneously at the bottom of the screen, urging viewers again to phone if they had any information.

Ryan flashed another white-on-white smile. "This is Ryan Velox from *Long Island Live*, signing off. Have a good night."

He waited until the cameras panned to another newscaster and then got out of his seat.

"Well?" he said to the crew. "What do you think?"

There was silence, then a huge burst of applause.

"Another fabulous job, Ryan," his producer crowed. "It's pretty much guaranteed WLIL's phones will be ringing off the hook this evening. You done us proud."

Ryan nodded. He'd sensed in his bones that he was on his way. Two more segments remained and then he would demand the coveted promotion. The anchor spot would be his. He deserved it. That plus a big fat raise.

Chapter 10

Kristie sat on Zan's sailboat, her feet dangling over the edge. Her face was tilted to the sun and she barely registered the peculiar gray green of Long Island Sound below as she tried to relax. A slightly overcast sky hinted that rain might be on the horizon.

She darted a glance at Zan, who was busy adjusting the sails. It was her first time out on a sailboat and she hadn't realized how luxurious they were. Zan's was polished mahogany and well appointed. The downstairs cabin had a living area that no doubt had been professionally decorated. Kristie had used the spacious bathroom to change into shorts and a T-shirt, clothing that Zan had lent her since she hadn't thought to bring her own. The jeans and sweatshirt she'd worn had grown impossibly warm.

Kristie had wondered where he'd acquired the clothes that fit her so perfectly. Then she'd concluded that they were leftovers from one of his admirers.

Zan's invitation to go sailing had come as a surprise since she hadn't known of the boat's existence until she got to his home. The refrigerator
in the dining area was stocked with food. She'd noticed when he opened the fridge and poured them
mimosas. The two drinks she'd had helped ease her
stress.

Zan came to sit beside her.

"Boat's anchored," he said.

Kristie could feel the heat coming off his skin as
he stuck out his powerful legs and wiggled his toes.
Golden hairs covered every inch of his body. In casual attire he looked awfully good.

A cap, the bill turned backward, covered his
shaved head, and a tiny gold hoop circled his earlobe. A cropped T-shirt exposed a glimpse of a flat
stomach. For at least the tenth time Kristie wondered how someone who looked like Zan remained
unattached.

"What did you think of Velox's broadcast last
night?" he asked, looking intently at her.

Kristie shrugged but remained noncommittal.
"I watched it at Lizette's. We thought he did a cred-
ible job. I can only hope that someone seeing it
might have news of Curtis."

"The program aired after dinner, a good time to
reach maximum viewers."

"What about our detective? Any word from him?"

Zan sipped from a tumbler. "Bill went back to the
airport and distributed copies of Earl's and Curtis's
photos. The woman who thought she saw Earl and
Curtis was sick. He plans on returning next week."

Kristie sighed. "So we have nothing." Her last
hope had just been dashed. "What about flight
records?"

Zan squeezed her hand. "Bill's still working on that. The cops should have something though. Haven't they spoken with you?"

"They've not been very communicative."

Zan's hand lingered in hers and Kristie held on to his rough palm as if it were a lifeline. There was something about T. Zan McManus that made her trust him and believe that he would do everything in his power to bring Curtis home. Time was no longer on her side. As the days slipped by, the odds of finding Curtis were reduced.

Kristie realized she'd remained numb through it all and had given up her power. A black hopelessness had swirled around her like a cloak and she needed to regain control. The moment she got home she would start passing out flyers to every living soul she came in contact with. She would also make the library her best friend and research everything there was to know about missing children. That would be her mission. The reason she lived.

"Hungry?" Zan asked, breaking into her thoughts.

"I'm starving."

"Then let's eat," he said, taking her hand.

Kristie followed Zan down the narrow stairway and into the cabin. He stopped briefly to turn on the stereo and pop in a Natalie Cole CD. The singer's sultry voice filled the small space as he led Kristie to a dining nook with two places already set.

Kristie eased into the banquette as Zan reached into the refrigerator. He returned to set down baguettes, a bowl of cold chicken salad, and a large plate of fruit. The pitcher of mimosas followed.

"I have iced tea," Zan said, "if you prefer."

"Do you have water?"

"Of course."

He retrieved miniature bottles of Evian from the refrigerator that seemed to hold everything short of the kitchen sink. Sliding into the booth across from her, Zan passed her the basket of baguettes.

Kristie spread chicken salad on the crusty roll and took her first bite. "Mmmm. This is delicious."

For the first time in a long time she actually tasted her food. She'd only eaten because she needed to keep up her strength, knowing that a sick mother would be useless to Curtis.

"I'm glad you came," Zan said, biting into his baguette.

"I'm glad I did too," Kristie agreed. Being out on the boat had almost helped take her mind off her troubles.

Initially she'd felt guilty sitting on Zan's luxurious boat. The alternative, however, held very little appeal. She would have been holed up in her house—providing she could get to it—with the media on her steps.

Kristie poured water into a glass and sipped. She eyed Zan surreptitiously over the rim. Anyone who didn't know their true relationship could easily mistake them for lovers except they were attorney and client and she meant to keep it like that.

She turned her attention to the fruit, took several nibbles, and then started on the chicken salad. Sated, she wiped her mouth on the linen napkin Zan had set next to her plate.

"There's dessert," he said, leaping up and heading for the refrigerator.

Kristie hugged her full stomach. "None for me, thanks."

"Coffee then? I make the best in the world."

"Coffee I'll have."

Zan left her to enter the small galley and returned with a pot. He poured two cups and they drank it without speaking.

What was Curtis doing right now? Kristie wondered. Had Earl become a responsible parent overnight? She'd fought so hard to show the judge that he was an unfit parent. But Earl's therapists at the outpatient-recovery program had claimed he was a changed man and had overcome his dependency. They'd convinced the judge that he was substance-free. Kristie hadn't fought the ruling.

She'd doubted that Earl was a changed man. He'd entered the rehabilitation program because he was smart. He knew the judge would look on it favorably, especially when he requested visitation rights. He'd gotten himself a job stocking shelves at a local grocery store. As predicted, that job didn't last.

If only she knew for certain that Curtis was being cared for. Kristie got out her cell phone and tried checking her messages. She had no service. She replaced the phone in her bag and sighed heavily.

"What are you thinking about?" Zan asked, breaking into her thoughts.

"My son. There's little else I think about these days."

"Tell me about Curtis."

"What is it you'd like to know?"

"Everything. Tell me about his personality. How he spends a typical day. That sort of thing."

Curtis was a favorite topic but speaking about him might make her sad. No sadder than she already was. What it might do was help release some of her pent-up angst.

"Curtis is beautiful inside and out. He's only about this high," Kristie said, placing a hand to indicate her shoulder. "And he's got a missing tooth. I paid him . . . rather the Tooth Fairy paid him five bucks for that tooth. He's full of energy and he's mischievous, but he's always sweet. He's a typical boy."

"Tell me more about him," Zan urged, appearing to be quite fascinated by what she was saying.

"Well, there was that time he found a baby mouse outside and brought it into the house. Of course he didn't tell me. He wrapped it in a towel and put it in a box in the bathroom. I damn near died when I stepped out of the shower and this thing went racing across the floor. I forgot about being naked, I opened that bathroom door and raced out screaming."

Kristie's hand clapped her mouth. She'd divulged too much. What could she be thinking about sharing a story like that? Zan might think she was coming on to him. She wasn't interested in coming on to anyone and most definitely not her attorney, as good looking as he was.

"And how did you get rid of the mouse?" Zan asked with a straight face.

"I managed to get some clothes on, then called one of the neighbors. The captured mouse was actually more scared than me."

"They usually are," Zan said dryly, the sides of his mouth quivering.

"What about you?" Kristie asked. "What were you like as a boy?"

"Hardheaded."

"You mean driven?"

"No, I mean hardheaded," Zan said. "I was raised

in the foster care system and adopted at age eight. I'd been told both parents had abandoned me and I acted out every chance I got. It was attention I craved."

"Oh, Zan, I'm sorry," Kristie said, truly feeling for him. She couldn't imagine what it must be like not having parents. Hers had retired to Florida but were always a phone call away and if she ever needed them they would be there. She'd already declined their offer to come and stay with her.

Zan stood abruptly, his jaw muscles working. "Nothing to be sorry about. I made out okay."

"How could parents leave you in foster care?"

"Easily. My father took off with me and when I became too much to care for he abandoned me. My mother claims she had no idea where we'd both disappeared to."

"You believe her?"

"She was a weak woman. My father had her pretty beaten down and she was afraid of him. Afraid of what he would do to her if she came after him or me."

Kristie could understand that. She'd been an abused woman with little self-esteem and few resources. It was easy to give in and do absolutely nothing rather than take a stand, especially when the stand you took ultimately brought with it pain. One night she'd gathered what little dignity she had left and called a crisis hot line. The counselor had literally saved her life.

Zan's fingers massaged his forehead. Kristie realized his admission had not come easily.

"I would move mountains to get Curtis back," she said out loud.

"You would still have to know where your child was to make that possible," Zan pointed out.

Saying Curtis's name made Kristie feel uncomfortable and guilty. She should check her messages and see if service was restored. She should make arrangements to have her phone calls forwarded to Mikaela when she was unavailable. She'd dragged her feet far too long.

Kristie stood, found her purse, rummaged through it, and removed her cell phone. She started up the stairs and onto the open deck. Maybe the phone would work up there.

A cool breeze ruffled her hair as she realized service was back. She punched in the requisite digits to retrieve messages and listened to reporters and well-wishers go on. Her parents had phoned and Mikaela, after her fourth phone call, sounded frantic.

"You must ring me the instant you get this."

The next message was filled with static. Kristie heard her son's voice over the crackle. Curtis sounded plaintive and needy and for one millisecond her heart stopped beating. She made out the words "artist island" over the static and that it wasn't fun. He badly wanted to come home. Kristie was elated to hear from him yet scared at the same time. She desperately wanted her son and not a disembodied voice.

The message ended and another began, but Kristie was no longer listening. She snapped off the phone and headed down the stairs. Zan was on his way up.

"What's happened?" he asked, grasping her by the shoulders and steadying her. Kristie was shaking. "What's going on?"

"C-C-Curtis called. He left a message."

"Let me listen," he said, grabbing for the phone.

Kristie managed to push the buttons again and press in the code. She turned the phone over to Zan.

"We need to get back and call the police immediately," he said, listening carefully and quietly, then handing her cell back and heading off to raise the anchor.

As soon as he tied up the boat, Kristie leapt off. They hurried up an azalea-lined path and into the house.

Zan called the Baldwin precinct while Kristie paced the living room floor. After the phone call was completed, he grabbed his car keys and said, "Let's go."

"You're coming with me?" Kristie asked, her eyes pooling with gratitude.

"Better believe I am. I'm following you home. You need an attorney. Any number of people will be looking for you. The police will want to hear the tape with Curtis's message."

"I suppose you're right."

Kristie made her wooden legs move. She picked up her pocketbook, dug for her car keys, and followed Zan out.

She settled into the driver's seat of her beat-up Toyota. It would be the longest ride that she would ever take home. What had Curtis meant when he said, "The artist island isn't fun"?

Kristie racked her brain but drew a blank. Zan patiently waited in the Lexus for her to start up the car. She turned the key and the engine coughed as it usually did, forcing her to step on the accelera-

tor. The vehicle lurched forward and she threw it
into reverse, backing out of Zan's winding driveway.

The ride to Baldwin took longer than it should.
Kristie was afraid to push the ailing car beyond the
speed limit. Frightening thoughts now crowded her
head. Her son had sounded so forlorn. Where was
his father? And where was this island of artists?

By the time she maneuvered her car into the
neighborhood, Kristie's temples pounded. Zan's
silver Lexus remained behind as she peered down
her street, noticing the van parked in front of her
house, and the handful of people camped on her
front steps, people she assumed were reporters.

She needed this like she needed a hole in the
head. She would park a block away in front of the
Brownes'. Zan brought the Lexus to a grinding halt
behind her, raced out, and rapped on her window.

Kristie lowered the window and jerked her thumb
in the direction of her house, silently communicating that she didn't want to deal with paparazzi.

"Let's go," Zan said, grabbing the Toyota's door
handle.

Kristie got out of her car and took Zan's hand,
twining their fingers together.

"There's got to be another way to get to your
house," he said, looking up and down the street.

"We'll go through a neighbor's backyard. We can
enter through the kitchen."

"Hurry then and let's try not to draw attention
to ourselves."

"We'll get arrested for trespassing," Kristie joked,
offering a tremulous smile.

The Fosters' house was directly in back of Kristie's,

An Important Message From The ARABESQUE Publisher

Dear Arabesque Reader,

Arabesque is celebrating 10 years of award-winning African-American romance. This year look for our specially marked 10th Anniversary titles.

Plus, we are offering *Special Collection Editions* and a *Summer Reading Series*—all part of our 10th Anniversary celebration.

Why not be a part of the celebration and let us send you four more specially selected books FREE! These exceptional romances will be sent right to your front door!

Please enjoy them with our compliments, and thank you for continuing to enjoy Arabesque.... the soul of romance bringing you ten years of love, passion and extraordinary romance.

Linda Gill
PUBLISHER, ARABESQUE ROMANCE NOVELS

P.S. Don't forget to check out our 10th Anniversary Sweepstakes—no purchase necessary—at www.BET.com

SPECIAL OFFER!
4 BOOKS FREE!

ARABESQUE
BET BOOKS

A SPECIAL "THANK YOU"
FROM ARABESQUE JUST FOR YOU!

Send this card back and you'll receive 4 FREE Arabesque Novels—a $25.96 value—absolutely FREE!

The introductory 4 Arabesque Romance books are yours FREE (plus $1.99 shipping & handling). If you wish to continue to receive 4 books every month, do nothing. Each month, we will send you 4 New Arabesque Romance Novels for your free examination. If you wish to keep them, pay just $16* (plus, $1.99 shipping & handling). If you decide not to continue, you owe nothing!

- Send no money now.
- Never an obligation.
- Books delivered to your door!

We hope that after receiving your FREE books you'll want to remain an Arabesque subscriber, but the choice is yours! So why not take advantage of this Arabesque offer, with no risk of any kind. You'll be glad you did!

In fact, we're so sure you will love your Arabesque novels, that we will send you an Arabesque Tote Bag FREE with your first paid shipment.

Call Us TOLL-FREE At
1-888-345-BOOK

* Prices subject to change

THE "THANK YOU" GIFT INCLUDES:

- 4 books absolutely FREE (plus $1.99 for shipping and handling).
- A FREE newsletter, *Arabesque Romance News*, filled with author interviews, book previews, special offers, and more!
- No risks or obligations. You're free to cancel whenever you wish with no questions asked.

INTRODUCTORY OFFER CERTIFICATE

Yes! Please send me 4 FREE Arabesque novels (plus $1.99 for shipping & handling). I understand I am under no obligation to purchase any books, as explained on the back of this card. Send my free tote bag after my first regular paid shipment.

NAME _____

ADDRESS _____ APT. _____

CITY _____ STATE _____ ZIP _____

TELEPHONE ( ) _____

E-MAIL _____

SIGNATURE _____

Offer limited to one per household and not valid to current subscribers. All orders subject to approval. Terms, offer, & price subject to change. Tote bags available while supplies last.

Thank You!

AN024A

ARABESQUE

Accepting the four introductory books for FREE (plus $1.99 to offset the cost of shipping & handling) places you under no obligation to buy anything. You may keep the books and return the shipping statement marked "cancelled". If you do not cancel, about a month later we will send 4 additional Arabesque novels, and you will be billed the preferred subscriber's price of just $4.00 per title. That's $16.00* for all 4 books for a savings of almost 40% off the cover price (Plus $1.99 for shipping and handling). You may cancel at any time, but if you choose to continue, every month we'll send you 4 more books, which you may either purchase at the preferred discount price. . . or return to us and cancel your subscription.

* PRICES SUBJECT TO CHANGE

THE ARABESQUE ROMANCE CLUB: HERE'S HOW IT WORKS

THE ARABESQUE ROMANCE BOOK CLUB
P.O. BOX 5214
CLIFTON NJ 07015-5214

and they raced through the backyard. They'd almost made it to the fence when the owner, Rebecca Foster, stuck her head out of a window and shouted, "Hey, Kristie, your block's swarming with people. I hope you find your son soon."

Rebecca's voice carried. Kristie waved a hasty acknowledgment and flipped the latch on her neighbor's gate. Just in time too, because pounding footsteps indicated someone was hot on their trail.

"Give me your key," Zan demanded, tugging Kristie along.

Kristie turned over her key and they raced across her scrap of backyard and up three little steps.

Shouts followed now.

"Ms. Phillips, I'm with the *Bugle*. I'd like to interview you."

"Come on, Kristie, this shouldn't take long."

"Who's the man with you, Ms. Phillips?"

Flashbulbs erupted behind them as they made it to the back door.

"Hurry," Kristie urged, "twist the key to the right, that usually does it."

The door gave just as the first reporter vaulted over the fence. Zan practically shoved Kristie inside. He double-locked the door and braced himself against it.

"Whew, that was close," he said, wiping his brow while Kristie gulped in air. "The police should be here shortly, better prepare yourself for them."

Kristie had the feeling she was going to need more than deep breaths to get through the upcoming ordeal. Even a month's supply of oxygen wouldn't be enough.

Chapter 11

The doorbell rang. Zan went off to answer it.

"It's the police," he said, after putting an eye to the keyhole.

"Might as well let them in."

Kristie lounged on the couch, two fingers massaging her aching temples. She was still casually attired in the T-shirt and shorts Zan had lent her. He opened the front door. Ed Sloan and his sidekick, Banks, came strolling in.

"Who's he?" Sloan asked in his usual cocky manner, jerking a thumb in Zan's direction.

"My attorney. T. Zan McManus, meet Detective Ed Sloan."

Sloan's gaze roamed over them. You could practically sense what he was thinking, the smirk on his face said it all. He grunted a greeting at Zan and both men sized each other up. Banks circled, testosterone pumping.

"Why would you need an attorney, Ms. Phillips?" Sloan asked, shooting Kristie a disarming smile.

"Why can't Ms. Phillips have her lawyer present?" Zan countered, flashing an equally phony smile. "I'm the one who called the precinct."

"Were you now?" Sloan's gaze slid over Kristie again, taking in her casual attire. "Looks like you two have been out having fun. What do you have for me?"

Kristie pointed to the answering machine where a red light blinked. "Curtis called while I was out. He left a message."

"We'll take that tape," Banks said, heading in the direction of the phone. "The FBI will probably want it as well."

"The FBI?" She hadn't thought of that.

"They're involved. We have proof that your child's been taken out of the country. We got the Mexicana passenger records."

"My son's in Mexico?"

Kristie's heart pounded and her chest felt tight. The FBI's involvement made it sound so official. Official and scary.

Banks removed the tape from the machine. "Do you have another to put in?" he asked.

Kristie simply nodded. The police had gotten what they'd come for and now she wished that they'd go.

"Anything else, boys?" Zan asked, making it clear they'd overstayed their welcome, and shooting a concerned look her way.

"We have what we need," Sloan answered, sauntering to the door. "You talk to your friend?"

"My friend as in Lizette?" Kristie managed to get out.

"Yeah, she's the only one I know."

COME BACK TO ME

"Not since yesterday."

"She tell you anything about us?"

Zan cleared his throat. "Is this official business, Officer Sloan, or personal chitchat?"

"I'm just making friendly conversation."

"Then maybe you should be on your way." Zan was basically throwing the detectives out.

Sloan slanted a challenging glance his way but to his credit continued out. He signaled Banks to follow. "We'll be in touch, Ms. Phillips," he said, then turned back. "I'm looking forward to your television interview."

Kristie mumbled something as the door shut behind them. She turned to find Zan standing there. He placed steadying arms around her and she leaned into him, welcoming his comforting presence.

Having Zan with her felt good.

"Damn it, old lady," Earl shouted, advancing on Senora Gonzalez. "You were supposed to be keeping an eye on my son."

"*Sí,* senor, *pero—*"

"But nothing." Earl utilized his limited knowledge of the Spanish he'd picked up to block the old bag's excuses.

"I left Curtis with you," he said, punching his fist into his open palm. "I told you you were not to let him out of your sight. I agreed to pay you extra to baby-sit. How could you be so stupid?"

Senora Gonzalez began to cry and wring her hands. "*Mi perro. Mi perro.*"

Her daughter, Esperanza, who'd been in the back room, rushed to her mother's side. "Pobrecito will be okay. We must find Curtis." She pointed a finger at Earl. "Why you make my mother cry?"

Earl ran ebony hands, made even darker by the sun, through wooly hair. "Because she's stupid. She was to watch Curtis and she allowed him to escape."

"My mother is not stupid," Esperanza ranted, getting into his face and wagging that finger at him. "We put up with your drinking and your pot smoking. We put up with you. Where else you going to find someone who charges so little, eh?"

Earl was not about to debate that point. He needed to find Curtis and fast, before the kid began flapping his gums. A black child of Curtis's age was bound to draw attention. Earl couldn't risk that.

"Ask your mother when she saw Curtis last," he said to Esperanza, in much calmer tones.

Esperanza began babbling to her mother in Spanish before turning back to Earl. "My mother said she last saw him this morning. He was watching television with the dog. Pobrecito's gone too."

Earl didn't give a damn about the mangy mongrel. He just needed to find his son. "And what time was that?"

Esperanza rambled to her mother in Spanish. "Mama says it was right before lunch."

Almost five hours ago. Valuable time had already been lost and the sun was going down.

"Why didn't she go out looking for him?"

"She thought he was walking the dog."

"For five hours?"

"My mother can barely walk herself. Look."

Earl stormed out of the house without answering. He started down the street, stopping to ask

the vendors who were packing up if they'd seen
Curtis. Most just shook their heads.

He approached a woman who sold papier-mâché
clowns and other colorful items and asked, "Have
you seen a little black boy about this high?" Earl
made a motion with his hand.

The vendor shaded her eyes and scrutinized Earl.
"Earlier I saw a little boy walking a dog."

"That would be Curtis. Which way was he heading?"

She pointed down the street. "He may have gone
into the stationer's shop on the corner."

"Thanks," Earl grunted, already loping away.

He arrived at the store as Mr. Santiago was closing up. The shopkeeper beamed at him.

"*Hola.* You looking for your little boy?"

"You've seen Curtis?"

"He came in with the dog and I gave him some
candy."

"And you didn't think to ask him what he was
doing out alone?"

Mr. Santiago scratched his head, ignoring Earl's
bunched fists. "I thought he was taking the dog
out for a walk."

Why was it everyone assumed it was okay for a
six-year-old boy to be out alone because he had a
dog with him?

"Which way was he heading when he left?" Earl
asked, guessing it would be virtually impossible to
catch up with Curtis now.

Santiago shrugged. "Don't know, but he was in a
hurry. He bought a phone card and I helped him
call the United States."

That probably meant Curtis had tried reaching

his mother again. The police might be hot on his trail as he stood questioning this idiot. It was time to move on. He'd have to find Curtis on his own. Kristie was probably raising an almighty ruckus.

Earl raced from the store and headed up the street. The effect of the pills that he'd gotten in return for delivering a gram of cocaine to a tourist was beginning to wear off. He needed to score soon, but his priority right now was to find Curtis.

Earl slowed down when he heard someone calling his name. He turned around to see Vic, the dealer, behind him.

"Hey, man. Why are you in such a hurry?" Vic asked.

"I'm looking for my son. He's lost."

Vic patted his knapsack and jutted his chin toward the alleyway. "I've got some really good stuff and I've got a proposition for you."

It sounded tempting, one quick hit and then he'd be on his way. Earl followed Vic into the alleyway where the dealer removed several zip-lock bags from his knapsack. He held them out to Earl to sniff. A craving kicked in, one that Earl could not control. It was irrelevant that he was low on funds. He needed something and he needed it now.

"Let me have a joint or two," Earl pleaded.

Vic reached into his bag and handed him two blunts. "Consider this an advance," he said. "I have another job for you."

Earl lit up a joint, drawing the smoke into his lungs. "All right, hit me."

The soothing herb went to work and Earl was willing to listen to Vic's proposal regardless of how outlandish it might be.

Vic gave him the specifics and mentioned an unbelievable sum for simply making the drop. It was the kind of money Earl needed to move on and set up house elsewhere.

Earl agreed to the terms. After Vic left, he leaned his back against the brick wall and finished the blunt. The life he'd created for himself wasn't half bad. He would love to stay on Isle de Artistes but couldn't since Curtis had disappeared. Damn that boy, he'd give him something to cry about when he got his hands on him.

The phone rang as Lizette stepped out of the shower. She made a face although there was no one to see it. She'd been thinking of going into Manhattan and had tried calling Kristie to see if she wanted to join her. No one answered and she wondered if her friend was still with Zan McManus.

"Yes?" Lizette inquired, one hand clutching the towel that was wrapped around her.

"How's my girl?"

Lizette recognized the deep voice as Ed's. Tremors of something she didn't care to identify skittered up her spine as he continued to talk.

"So what you been up to?"

"I'm getting ready to go out," Lizette answered, ticked that he'd waited until now to call.

"You going somewhere without me?"

"You're supposed to be working."

"Yeah, but I get off at ten. Come over to my place."

"I don't know where you live," Lizette reminded him.

Ed gave her an address in Oceanside and Lizette

looked around for a pen and paper to scribble it down.

"I'll pick up some wine and we can listen to tunes," he said, sounding both cocky and confident.

He was taking it for granted that she was going to drop everything and come over to his home after work. The truth was she had nothing better to do and she did want to see Ed Sloan.

Memories of their last time together made Lizette blush and clutch her towel more tightly. Ed had been an expert lover. He'd been both thoughtful and caring. But he'd taken his time about getting back in touch.

"I'll see you at ten-thirty then," he said and waited.

"Yes, you'll see me."

Lizette hung up, mad at herself. This was obviously a booty call. She cautioned herself not to take him seriously.

In the couple of hours she had to get ready, Lizette treaded a path to her closet and back again. She tried on a dozen outfits, then discarded them. She needed something slinky and sexy that would camouflage her hips. An hour later she settled on a black dress with a plunging neckline, which she would wear with silver jewelry. Lizette piled her hair high on her head, secured it with pins, and went to work on her face. When she was through she had about a half hour at her disposal. It was time to try reaching Kristie again.

Kristie's machine picked up and Lizette began leaving a message. Her friend's voice interrupted.

"Sorry, I'm screening calls."

"I was getting worried," Lizette admitted. "It's been a while since I've heard from you. How did your day with Zan go?"

"Zan's still here," Kristie whispered.

"How come? You two doing the nasty?" It was meant as a joke but Lizette wondered why an attorney was baby-sitting his client at this late hour. On the other hand the relationship between Zan and Kristie had been odd from the beginning.

Kristie ignored the lurid comment. "It's been quite the day," she said. "I've had reporters camped on my doorstep and the police were here, your man, Ed."

"Ed was at your place? Why? What happened?"

A beat, then two went by. Kristie seemed to catch her breath. "I got a message from Curtis."

"Oh, Kristie, that's fabulous news. Where is he? Is he on his way home?"

This time there was an audible gulp. "I don't know. I'll tell you the story when I see you. Right now I'm throwing clothes in a bag."

"Are you coming over here?" Lizette asked, already mentally preparing to cancel on Ed.

"No. Uh, Zan invited me to stay with him until things cool off."

"You think that's such a hot idea?"

"I can't think of a better one. I need to be someplace the press can't find me. Ride around my neighborhood and you'll see why it's a very good idea. We'll talk later."

Kristie hung up and the dial tone resounded in Lizette's ear. Lizette decided the whole world was going crazy. She was heading over to a man's apartment at a strange hour, one she barely knew. And normally cautious Kristie was moving in with her attorney.

Regardless of whether the relationship was platonic or not, it was all too weird.

Chapter 12

"Where are your parents, little boy?" a woman in a funny white dress asked. She carried two grocery bags, each balanced on a hip.

Curtis looked up at the woman, who looked like a walking tent, but couldn't think of a quick enough answer. The lady had a kind face and she smiled at him. Curtis wondered whether he should tell her that he was trying to get home to his mother and that he'd lost Pobrecito.

"I don't know where my dad is," Curtis finally admitted.

She bent down and her long braids covered her shoulders. "What's your name, son?"

"Curtis."

"Does Curtis have a last name?"

Curtis thought for a moment. His mother had taught him not to lie, but she'd also told him he shouldn't speak to strangers. "Leone," he mumbled, hanging his head.

"You're awfully young to be on the streets by yourself," the woman said, making a face. "I don't understand why adults are so irresponsible these days."

A tear slid down Curtis's face and then another and another. "I was walking my dog and I lost him," he said. "Pobrecito has my belt around his neck. He's black and brown and really skinny."

The lady thought for a while. She shifted her paper bags and settled them more securely on her hips. "I haven't seen your dog," she admitted, "but it's getting dark soon. Hop into my truck and I'll drop you off near the police station. They'll help you find your father."

Curtis's mother had warned him not to get into cars driven by strangers. She'd said that would be a dangerous thing to do. She'd told him that people stole children. His father also hated the police. He'd told Curtis they were bad. He couldn't get into a truck with this woman, kind as she looked.

"I can't go with you," Curtis said firmly.

The woman threw her head back and laughed. The beads attached to her braids banged together, then separated. Curtis thought it was strange that she wore a hairstyle like the neighborhood teenagers that sometimes baby-sat him. But she seemed like a really nice woman and Curtis could tell she wanted to help.

When she finally stopped laughing she said, "And why can't you go with me?"

"Because you're a stranger, and my mom said never to get into a car with strangers."

His answer made the woman laugh even more. Curtis thought he'd never met an adult who laughed so easily.

"What if I told you my name?" she said. "We wouldn't be strangers anymore and maybe you'd come with me."

"Maybe."

It was getting dark and Curtis was scared and getting more scared by the moment. The darkening sky looked like it held rain and he knew he couldn't go back to the boardinghouse. His father would be angry and would hit him. Senora Gonzalez would be upset because he'd lost her dog. Maybe he should let the woman tell him her name.

"Moonbeam," she said, holding out her hand to him.

Curtis shook it as he'd been taught to do. Moonbeam was the strangest name. "Mine is Curtis Leone," he said.

Moonbeam cocked her head to the side, studying him, and after a while said, "I like your name. It sounds like you're going places, young man."

Curtis beamed at her.

"Want to help me with one of my packages?"

"Sure."

Moonbeam gave him one of her packages, which really wasn't very heavy. It was filled with paper goods. They began walking up the street toward a purple pickup truck with orange polka dots painted on the doors. The truck looked like something Curtis had seen in a cartoon.

"Now let's see," Moonbeam said, studying him. "I could probably drop you off near the police station as I promised. But I've got to be sure the pigs don't see me. I've been fined twice and I refuse to pay. The police don't like me and they hate the Purple People Eater." She patted the hood of the truck.

"Your truck's called the Purple People Eater?" Curtis made a face, then began to laugh.

"Yes, it is." His comment didn't seem to bother Moonbeam a bit.

Curtis couldn't stop laughing. He'd never met anyone who named their truck.

"My dad doesn't like the police either," he admitted. "He wouldn't be happy if you left me with them. I'll probably get a beating."

"Your father hits you?" Moonbeam said, sounding like it was the worst thing she'd heard.

"Only when I'm bad. I try not to do anything to make him mad," Curtis said, hanging his head. "I ran away today."

"I'd run away too if anyone laid a hand on me," Moonbeam muttered, screwing up her face and looking as if she wanted to hit someone. "I suppose I could take you home with me and then we can both decide what to do."

Curtis climbed into her truck. She backed it out of its parking place, speeding down the road as if she were being chased by a hundred Pobrecitos. They were soon in the countryside and the Purple People Eater groaned as they started up a mountain.

"Do you live up there?" Curtis asked, pointing to the top.

"Yes, I have a little house that I rent. It's not much but I don't have neighbors and that's the way I like it. I came here to paint, that's how I earn my living. You'll see how beautiful and peaceful it is when we get there."

Curtis's eyelids felt heavy. Moonbeam had the window down and the cool breeze drifting in made

him sleepy. He sat back and relaxed and forgot about
his father.

A hand touched his shoulder. "Wake up, Curtis.
We're here." Curtis jumped. He must have fallen
asleep and been dreaming. He'd thought he was
home in his bed and that his mother was saying it
was time for school. He opened his eyes and saw
Moonbeam standing in front of a little wooden
house that needed paint.

"Is this your home?" he asked.

"Yes, this is my palace," Moonbeam said, waving
her hands in the direction of the house.

Curtis picked up one of Moonbeam's packages
and slid out of the passenger seat. She was already
at her door. She kicked off her sandals and gestured to Curtis to remove his sneakers. Together
they entered the tiny home.

The living room had colorful pillows on the floor
and paintings of what looked like jungle scenes.
They entered a tiny kitchen and Moonbeam opened
cabinet doors and took out several candles.

"I have no electricity," she said. "It will soon be
dark. Help me light them."

So Curtis did. He'd never been in a house without electricity but he liked Moonbeam's tiny home.
He watched as she unpacked her groceries and
made space for them in the cabinets.

"I suppose we should figure out what we're going
to do about dinner," she said after a while. "I don't
eat meat. I'm a vegetarian."

Moonbeam poured Curtis a drink that she claimed to have made from wild berries and watched him

drink. When he was done she said, "Curtis, would you like to spend the night with me? Tomorrow when the mailman comes we'll get a message to your mother. You do have a mother?"

"Yes, she's in the United States."

Moonbeam's fingers stroked her chin. "Your father is probably worried about you."

Curtis wasn't so sure his father was worried; more likely he was mad. He decided to stay quiet and let Moonbeam come up with a plan. He was still worried about Pobrecito and hoped the dog had found his way home, just as he needed to find his way home.

Moonbeam began to make them dinner. Curtis sat on the floor watching her. It was the first time that he had felt safe since coming to the Island of Artists. It was the first time he felt at home.

Ed opened his door to Lizette and leered at her. He was bare-chested and had a towel draped around his neck.

"Hey, sweet thing," he said, kissing her. "You look good enough to eat." He stepped back and his eyes swept her cleavage.

"Are you planning on asking me in?" Lizette said while Ed continued to stare.

"Of course." He stood aside, allowing her to enter. "Come on in."

Lizette's eyes lingered on Ed's wide chest and the thick hairs covering his pectorals.

"I just got in ten minutes ago," he admitted. "I was about to take a shower."

"Don't let me stop you," she said, looking around for a place to sit.

"I was hoping that you'd join me." One hand cupped her butt. He gave it a little squeeze. "Come on, hon."

Lizette wanted to tell him that he was taking a lot for granted, but then she remembered how good he made her feel. Ed knew how to push all of her hot buttons, and she had agreed to come to his apartment. She wanted the same thing as he did.

He drew her into the apartment and gave her a floor-tilting kiss. Lizette was out of the black dress quicker than she expected. She stood in her black thong panties. The dress would have been ruined by a panty line.

"Wow!" Ed said, eyeing her appreciatively. He took her hand and tugged her through the apartment and into his bedroom. He stopped briefly to shed his jeans and she noticed he wore no underwear. His large hands circled her waist and he lifted her up and carried her into a bathroom that smelled of testosterone and him.

The black and cream tile walls held no paintings. A fluffy black and cream rug covered the floor and a full array of toiletries covered every inch of counter space.

Ed set Lizette down in front of a floor-length mirror and rested his chin on her shoulder. The other hand slid under her underwear, cupping her butt again.

"Look at how beautiful you are. Look at how beautiful we are together." His hand crept up to circle her breast. He nibbled on her earlobe, then blew a moist breath against her neck.

Butterflies fluttered in her belly and a throbbing began in her core. She wanted Ed to touch her all over and make her forget that she felt fat. Ed's erection pulsed against her buttocks and she felt she could grow wings and soar.

He left her briefly to step into the shower and turn on the water. When he returned, a misty fog filled the room, blurring their reflection. Hands still on her buttocks, he practically shoved her under the hot shower.

Ed's hands kneaded and massaged every inch of exposed skin. He suckled her nipples and backed her up against the wall. One hand reached for a bottle of liquid soap. He poured it into his palm and began rubbing it all over her.

"What about a condom?" she asked, beginning to relax.

"In the shower?"

Ed knelt between her legs as water poured down on his head. His tongue began probing and prying.

Lizette's feet arched and her toes curled. She held on to Ed's hair and stood on tiptoe as he continued to love her, making little mewling sounds that she could not control. A scream ripped through her as she finally let go and soared. Ed scooped her up and stepped out of the shower. He slid a condom on and drove into her. Lizette shuddered as he bit down on her shoulder, his bites becoming fiercer with each new thrust. Lizette's breasts banged against his chest and her head lolled back as she gave in to the feeling and let go.

The misty bathroom made Lizette feel as if she were sealed off from a world that consisted only of Ed.

"God, baby, you're good," Ed gasped.

His lust-filled eyes and sharp intakes of breath

made her feel powerful and in control. She clamped him firmly between her thighs and heard him groan.

"I stopped by Kristie's house earlier," he gasped, continuing to thrust.

Why was he fixated on her friend?

Ed gave another thrust and Lizette exploded. It felt as if she'd shoot right over Ed's shoulder, hit the wall, and happily die.

"Your Ms. Phillips doesn't know this yet," Ed said, "but her son might be in Mexico."

A part of Lizette's brain processed the information but she couldn't really concentrate. She was already halfway over the moon and Ed's talk of Mexico threatened to ground her.

"He's at this place called Isle de Artistes," Ed grunted before exploding inside her.

Lizette made a mental note to share this information with Kristie just before another orgasm ripped through her.

Chapter 13

Kristie surveyed the spacious suite that Zan had insisted she have. Her unpacked suitcase of clothing sat on the huge brass bed as she wandered around. It had been an impulsive decision, agreeing to stay with Zan. But the truth was she knew she was safe here. Reporters weren't likely to show up at an attorney's house on the tip of Long Island.

Staying at Mikaela's was the alternative, but commuting from New Jersey to make the daily trip to her job would be added stress. Kristie had also been reluctant to impose on Lizette. No one deserved to have their neighborhood turn into a media circus, least of all her friend.

After a late dinner, which Zan had ordered in, he'd excused himself, claiming that he needed to prepare for an upcoming case. Kristie had been left with little choice but to retreat to the room with the huge window walls overlooking Long Island Sound.

She focused on the business of unpacking, stepped into the spacious walk-in closet, and began hanging her clothes. Her calls had been forwarded to her cell phone and tomorrow Mikaela had agreed to pick them up.

Kristie could kick herself for not having forwarded her calls sooner. Had she, she wouldn't have missed Curtis's earlier phone call. Thinking of her son brought tears to her eyes. She hoped the police could piece together the clues and get back to her soon.

She changed into sweats and selected a magazine from the pile on the desk, then slid under the covers prepared to read until she fell asleep. Her cell phone rang just as she'd gotten comfortable. She jumped out of bed and raced to retrieve it.

"Hello," she said breathlessly.

"Kristie? Did I wake you?"

It was Lizette.

"I was planning on reading before I turned in," she said and waited.

"I have news that might interest you." Lizette sounded excited.

"I'm all ears. Talk to me."

"I just got back from Ed's," Lizette gushed. "He thinks that Curtis might be on this island in Mexico called Isle de Artistes."

"Mexico," Kristie repeated, her hands clutching her chest.

"Yes, in an artists' colony."

Maybe the police had something. Curtis had mentioned an artists' island in his garbled message.

"Why didn't Ed call me immediately?" Kristie asked. "He must know I'd want to hear this."

"Ed planned on telling you first thing tomorrow. Your phone tape was turned over to the FBI."

"You seem to know a lot. More than me," Kristie huffed. "And I'm Curtis's mother."

Lizette swallowed loudly. "I thought you would be happy about the news. I'll let you get back to whatever you were doing."

"Oh, Lizette, don't be mad," Kristie said, regretting her outburst. She hadn't meant to be ungracious. "I appreciate the heads-up. You're a good friend."

"Funny, but I don't feel like one," Lizette said, ending the conversation.

Kristie knew Lizette was annoyed. She'd make it up to her tomorrow.

News like this was too important to keep to herself. Kristie wandered downstairs and into the family room where she'd left Zan but he had already gone to bed.

Retracing her steps, she made her way down a long hallway and knocked on the first door. Getting no answer she turned the doorknob, flipped on the light, and peeked in.

A huge cranberry bathroom held a gigantic Roman tub with gold spigots. A gilt mirror adorned a far wall and fluffy cranberry and pink towels hung from the towel bars. On another wall a painting of a Nubian woman balanced a pot on her head.

Plush carpeting muffled her footsteps as she continued down the hall. Kristie tapped lightly on each of the closed doors. At the end of the hallway she took a deep breath and raised a hand to knock. The door flew open and Zan stood before her rubbing his eyes and smothering a yawn.

"What's wrong?" he asked, yawning again.

Kristie's eyes were drawn to his bare chest covered with hairs. She wanted to lay her head on its breadth and forget why she was here. It was sinful for a man to look so good.

"Lizette called," Kristie jabbered.

One of Zan's eyebrows rose sky-high. "What did she want?"

Kristie's face warmed. She was making a complete fool of herself. "Sloan thinks he knows where Curtis is."

Zan ran a hand over his shaved scalp. "Come in and give me a minute to wash my face."

Normally Kristie would have declined such an invitation but these weren't normal times.

She slid by Zan, entering a bedroom that was almost the size of her house. Zan disappeared into the bathroom and she used that time to gaze around her. A gigantic bed with a black wrought-iron headboard and gold knobs held huge pillows. A sound system took up one wall, and a picture window with a comfortable seat gave a nice view of the sound. But it was the unlit marble fireplace that drew her.

Kristie placed a hand on the mantel, fingering the sheer material that was the same as that bordering the windows. She wondered if the house was the work of a swanky designer.

Footsteps sounded behind her and she turned to see Zan approaching, pulling a T-shirt over his head.

"The fireplace was the reason I bought the house," he said when his head emerged.

Holding on to her hand, he led her to the sitting area. "Now back to Curtis."

Kristie repeated her conversation with Lizette.

"Isle de Artistes," Zan repeated. "I wonder why Sloan didn't call you himself." His voice dripped with disdain.

"We have to do something," Kristie said, rising and pacing.

"I'll get Bill on the horn first thing tomorrow. He needs to jump on this."

Kristie came to the sudden decision it was time to take control. "I'm asking for a leave of absence and I'm going to Mexico," she said resolutely.

"You want to think about this."

"Not much to think about. The police say my son is in Mexico. I'm not going to sit here and wait until they find him."

"Atta girl," Zan said, standing and wrapping his arms around her.

Kristie was suddenly cognizant of the late hour and of the masculine smell of the man holding her close. She should put a safe distance between them and not allow him to hold her hand, even if holding on to him was the only lifeline she had.

Zan kissed her cheek. "I'm coming with you."

"How can you?" she asked, looking at him in wonder.

"I own my own practice. I have no one to answer to."

"But you must have cases that require your attention."

"Yes, but with the exception of tomorrow, I have no trials scheduled for several weeks."

"The police aren't going to like this one bit," Kristie said reflectively.

"The police are hardly our concern. Unless you're

formally accused of something they can't stop us from getting on a plane and going to Mexico."

Zan kissed her on the lips this time, and Kristie kissed him back.

"I shouldn't have done that," he said, stepping away. "Sorry."

Kristie wasn't the least bit sorry. Even though she sensed that there was no place in his life for a lowly schoolteacher, kissing Zan McManus felt right. He certainly didn't need a single mom who didn't have two pennies to rub together. Still, the only thing that mattered now was finding her son. And Zan had agreed to help her do so.

Earl stood in the alleyway waiting for the tourist to come by and pick up the package. Vic had told him he was to collect cash, five hundred big ones, before turning the merchandise over. Twenty percent of the take would be his, and Earl could definitely use the money. The last of his cash had been spent at the bar. He would continue looking for Curtis after he'd concluded this business.

A rustling sound got Earl's attention. He jumped back as two rats scurried from a nearby cardboard box. They began to play hide-and-seek, chasing up and down the alley. Earl shuddered.

Twenty minutes passed and the effects of the beer and joints were beginning to wear off. Earl needed a pick-me-up and the temptation to open the package and sniff was getting to be too much to resist.

Footsteps sounded, then went by. Tourists greeted each other, heading for dinner. Earl could hear the street vendors packing up, slamming their items into rickety trucks.

Another five minutes went by, then ten. Earl gave in to the urge, inserted a fingernail under the sealed brown package, and opened it. From the feel he'd concluded cocaine. It had been a long time since he'd snorted that stuff. It was too expensive and his money didn't stretch that far.

He withdrew a small zip-lock bag, snapped on a penlight, and examined the contents. As he'd suspected, the bag was filled with a white powdery substance. Earl took a pinch between thumb and index finger before snorting it up. Numbness settled on the roof of his mouth and tongue, and an acrid liquid dripped down his throat. A feeling of elation and euphoria soon followed.

Earl zipped up the bag and resealed the package. It wasn't exactly in the same state he'd gotten it in, but anyone with common sense would want to see what they were buying. The penlight remained on.

The pungent odor in the alleyway no longer mattered. Earl placed a sneakered foot on the wall and contemplated his life. Several more minutes went by before he heard a whispered conversation and saw two burly men heading his way. Neither of them looked like the executive Vic promised, nor had he mentioned that the man would have someone with him.

"Yo, anyone there?" the inquiry came.

Earl snapped the penlight off, then on. The two men picked through the debris and headed his way. They were dressed in jeans and T-shirts. Earl ignored the uneasy feeling that was beginning to surface. The men were on holiday. The transaction would be over in minutes. Money would change hands. That's all that mattered now.

"What you got for me?" one of the men asked, coming closer.

"What you got for me?" Earl countered, remembering Vic's warning. Money first or no deal.

The man who'd remained silent withdrew several hundred-dollar bills and began counting. The other, clearly nervous, looked up the alleyway and began circling. Earl held out the brown package but made sure to keep a firm grip on it. The tourist had finished counting.

"Open it up," the man ordered. "We'll check just to make sure it's legit."

Earl swung the beam of the flashlight on the package. For the second time that night he opened it up. The circling man was in back of him now and Earl had the weird feeling that something wasn't right.

The talking man dipped a finger into the bag and held it up to the light.

"Looks authentic," he confirmed.

"Now that you've checked it out, pay me and it's yours," Earl said, wanting to hightail it out of there.

A hand clamped down on his wrists, twisting them, and the package fell to the ground.

"You're under arrest," the previously silent man barked as cold iron handcuffs were snapped into place.

The man in front of Earl flashed a badge. The alleyway was suddenly flooded with light and the sounds of sirens filled the night. Earl had been betrayed. Set up.

Reality hit home as he was led away. There was

nothing he could do now about finding his son. Even if he was allowed the obligatory phone call, he sure as hell couldn't call Kristie. He'd failed as a father and as a man.

Chapter 14

"Henry, get out here and see this," Jude Martin screeched. She'd been watching Ryan Velox's broadcast when it struck her that she had seen one of the little boys. A neighbor had called and suggested she tune in to the show and she'd been sitting spellbound ever since until that little boy's face had flashed on the screen. Then bingo, it hit. Jude could kick herself for missing the first segment. The child was the boy Kevin had played with in Mexico.

"I knew it. I knew it!" Jude yelled. "Come on, Henry, come on out here now."

Henry, who was in the shower, shouted back, "Unless it's an emergency or someone died I'll be there as soon as I can."

Jude sat on the edge of her sofa as photo after photo of missing children flashed on the screen. And the host Ryan Velox introduced the families. She was fascinated and at the same time horrified. She watched and listened to the stories of the loved ones that had disappeared. Many were now feared dead.

Jude had been especially captivated by Kristie Phillips's story and admired that she was a special ed teacher. Her Kevin had had his share of problems. He suffered from attention deficit disorder, which hadn't been diagnosed immediately. But with the aid of a specially trained teacher he'd now been able to focus.

The camera panned to Curtis Leone again, and Jude was certain that he was the little boy who'd played soccer with Kevin, the one they'd taken back to their hotel with them. Jude's fingers were itching to pick up the phone and call that 800 number Ryan Velox kept repeating, but then Henry might not want to get involved. She needed to talk to him.

Her husband had told her she had a tendency to mind other people's business. But this was different. It wasn't a case of simply being nosy. A little boy was missing, one she was certain she'd seen and spoken to. She'd even had the boy in her care. Jude felt for the mother. She herself was a mother after all.

"Henry," Jude called again, "please get out here before the program ends."

"I'm not interested in watching a sitcom," Henry answered. "I'll get out as soon as I can."

"Come on, Henry, please. This is important."

Henry eventually stomped out, hair damp, and still buttoning his shirt. "All right, this better be good."

Jude pointed to the screen. Ryan Velox was in the midst of urging viewers to call if they had any information at all.

Kevin, hearing his father, bounced out of his bedroom. He'd been playing Game Boy and still held the video game. He sat gingerly on the couch, one eye on the gadget, the other on the father he adored.

"What's this about?" Henry grumbled.

Jude began to fill him in. "You remember the little boy Kevin played soccer with on Isle de Artistes?"

"The one whose father stiffed me," Henry muttered. It was still a sore point.

"You mean Curtis," Kevin added. "I liked him."

"Yes, Curtis. Looks like he's a missing child," Jude said, pointing to the screen again. "Look, Henry. Look. Didn't I tell you something was funny?"

Henry sat on the couch and squinted at the television while photos of the missing children flashed on the screen again.

"Sure looks like him," he said grudgingly.

"That's him. That's Curtis," Kevin squealed, forgetting about the computer gadget for a moment.

"I'm calling the police," Jude said, springing up and heading for the phone.

"If anyone's calling anyone, I'll do it," Henry said, taking over. "There was something about that child's father that put me off. I mean, what responsible adult would leave his son unattended? Plus he was grimy and unkempt. Jude, did you notice how unfocused his eyes were?"

"Yeah, I thought maybe he was on drugs. But what could we do? We were visitors in a strange country and had no claim to that child."

"Okay, I'm calling the police. Give me that phone number again." Henry held the receiver in one hand, prepared to punch in numbers.

Jude rattled off the 800 number and Henry

plugged it in. After a while he was connected to an operator who passed him on to a detective. Henry told the detective what little he knew. Fifteen minutes later, after extracting a promise from the detective to let him know the minute Curtis was found, he was finally off the phone.

"Well?" Jude said. "Don't keep me in suspense. What did they say?"

"Not much. They were appreciative that I called. The detective wants me to stay in touch. He gave me his phone number."

Jude's face crumbled. A tear slid down her cheek. "I just hope to God that mother is able to find her son in one piece."

"I hope so too." Henry looked over at his own son, who was back to playing his game. "It must be hell not knowing where your child is."

Jude didn't even want to imagine what the young mother must be going through. Somehow she would find a way to reach her and share what little she knew. She'd do so with, or without, Henry's consent.

Zan pressed the intercom button and waited for his assistant to pick up.

"Miriam, can you get in here, please?"

Miriam hustled in, pad in hand, prepared to take notes.

"Please reschedule all of this week's appointments," Zan directed before she could sit down.

Miriam's eyebrows rose slightly. "This must be an emergency."

"You can call it that. I've got business that will take

me out of town. You can reach me on my international cell phone should something come up."

Miriam looked at him but it was hard to assess what she was thinking. After a while she said, "Kristie Phillips has been trying to reach you. She called several times. She's reachable after four. She did say she was able to get a leave of absence and she's working on purchasing a ticket to . . ." Miriam referred to the notepad she was carrying. "Isle de Artistes."

"Did she say she actually purchased an airline ticket?" Zan asked, reaching for his cell phone and punching in some numbers.

"She said she was working on it."

"Please call Mexicana Airlines and book us two seats in business class. Charge them to the corporate account. I'll get Ms. Phillips on the phone."

"She did say she wasn't available until after four," Miriam reminded him.

Zan nodded, dismissing her. "We'll see about that."

A mechanical voice responded to his query for the Learning Center's number. Zan punched in the digits and reached the administrative office. He asked to speak with Kristie Phillips.

"Ms. Phillips is in class," the secretary responded. "Is this urgent or is this something I can help you with?"

"I'd like Ms. Phillips, please. And yes, it's important."

Zan was left holding the line for a full ten minutes. It gave him time to think about what he was about to do. Finding Curtis Leon was important to him and in fact it had become a crusade. He'd begun to get flashbacks of the young boy he'd been, abandoned and left alone in a rooming house. It was the owner who'd called a child welfare center and from there he'd eventually been placed in foster care. Kristie finally came on the line sounding frantic.

"This is Kristie Phillips."

"Kristie, it's Zan."

"Is something wrong? Did we find Curtis?"

"No, hon. I'm checking to see if you already bought your plane ticket."

"I borrowed money from my sister but I'm still shopping for the right fare."

"Stop shopping. My assistant's getting us seats on Mexicana in business class."

"I can't afford business class," Kristie protested. "I can barely afford coach."

"All you need to worry about is packing clothes and a passport. You do have a passport?"

There was a pause. "Yes, I had planned on taking Curtis away this summer," Kristie admitted. "Lizette has the key to my house. She'll brave the reporters and get me clothes."

"I won't be home until late. I need to wrap up a few things. Will you be up?"

"I'll make it my business to be," Kristie said. "And, Zan, thanks again. You have no idea how much I appreciate everything you've done. You're not just an attorney but my very good friend."

Zan wanted to be more than Kristie's friend and attorney. But now wasn't the best time to make his move.

* * *

Kristie had just returned to her classroom when there was a knock on the door.

A substitute teacher entered. "I've been asked to take over for you. You're wanted in administration again."

Kristie made a face.

The substitute shrugged.

The classroom broke into excited chatter.

Kristie gave the children an assignment and instructed the aide to make sure the work was done. She hurried down the hallway wondering what this was about. Her steps picked up as she thought about forwarding her phone. Maybe someone had called Mikaela with a lead.

Kristie entered the office and the secretary looked up from her computer and offered a tentative smile. "This must be your day for phone calls," she said.

Kristie could think of no quick comeback but it didn't seem to matter.

"We've had every reporter you can think of call. A woman's on line two. She says it's urgent."

Kristie's heart pounded. She accepted the receiver with a sweaty palm. "This is Kristie Phillips."

"Ms. Phillips?" It wasn't Mikaela.

"Yes?"

"My name is Jude Martin."

Was that supposed to ring a bell? She waited for the woman to go on.

"I listened to last night's broadcast," she said.

Kristie held her breath while her stomach convulsed.

"The newscaster mentioned you were a special ed teacher. My son's had his problems, so I called all the schools I knew of to see if you worked there. I got lucky on the last number."

"What is it?" Kristie asked sharply. "What do you want?" Surely the woman wasn't looking for some-one to tutor her son.

"My family and I were on vacation in Mexico. We may have seen your boy."

"Oh, my God," Kristie said, clutching her chest as the room spun around her. "You saw Curtis?"

"We think we did. My husband called the number listed on the broadcast last night and spoke to a detective. Your kid, at least I believe it was your kid, played soccer with my little boy. We took him back to our hotel when the game was done. There wasn't an adult to claim him."

Kristie felt the air wheezing out of her lungs. "My son is in Mexico by himself?"

"Well, no. His father came by the hotel to pick him up. We thought it seemed strange, but there are so many single parents raising children these days that we turned him over without question."

"Describe the boy and his father, please," Kristie got out.

Jude Martin provided a detailed description of adult and child.

"Did the little boy have a missing tooth?"

"Yes, he did."

"That's Curtis," Kristie said, feeling faint. "That's my little boy. Give me your phone number. Did your husband tell this to the police?"

"Yes, he did."

And the bastards still hadn't called. The secretary, who'd obviously been listening, silently handed

Kristie a page from a legal pad. Kristie scribbled the woman's number down.

"Ms. Martin, can we meet? I get off of work in a couple of hours." There was a pause and Kristie pressed on. "I really would like to meet you in person."

"Henry, my husband, will probably think I'm getting overly involved."

"You're a mother," Kristie cried. "Imagine how you would feel if you couldn't find your son. I'm begging you, please."

That did it.

"We don't have to meet at your home," Kristie cried. "We can meet at a restaurant, any place that's convenient for you."

Jude Martin mentioned a well-known chain restaurant in Massapequa, adding, "It has to be before seven, before my husband gets home. I'm going to have to bring my son, Kevin, with me."

"I'll be there," Kristie answered, "and I'll bring a photo of Curtis with me."

Clutching the receiver, she stood catching her breath. The secretary went to the watercooler and poured her a cup of water. She handed it to her.

Kristie drank and drank. She needed to get back to her classroom before the substitute was driven crazy. She'd call Zan later from her cell phone and tell him what had transpired. She needed his strong shoulders and needed his support.

Curtis awoke to a sound outside his window that sounded like nothing he'd ever heard. Curiosity got the better of him and he rubbed his eyes and leapt out of bed. What he saw made him smile. A mother goat was leading two baby goats around the backyard. Every now and then they would raise their heads, open their mouths, and "maaaaa."

The only times Curtis had seen goats were on trips to the zoo, or when his school took him on a field trip to a farm. Now he couldn't wait to go outside and play with them.

His door creaked open and Moonbeam stuck her head inside.

"Hey, you," she said. "Hungry?"

He was starving.

"Clean up and I'll make you breakfast," Moonbeam said, placing a towel and what looked to be a new T-shirt on his bed. "Make it quick and you can help me collect the eggs we're having for breakfast."

Curtis had never heard of anyone collecting eggs. Eggs you bought at a supermarket, but Moonbeam made it sound like they were going to go on an Easter hunt just like he was used to doing with his mother.

She pointed him toward the one bathroom and showed him how to use the bucket of water she'd left there to clean up. The cabin didn't have running water and Curtis was beginning to think of this as a little adventure. His new friend Moonbeam was fun.

After using a sponge to take a quick wash he entered the kitchen to find Moonbeam fixing fresh vegetables she said they were going to have for lunch.

She poured him a glass of milk and Curtis, who normally didn't like milk, took a small sip.

"Mmmm, this is good," he said, making his eyes wide.

"I milked the goat. Goat milk is good for you, makes up for the vitamins you would normally have."

"Are the goats yours?" Curtis asked. He'd never heard of anyone owning their own goats, much less milking one.

Moonbeam shook her head. "No, they came with the place. They're wild but they make good company. They don't talk back."

"Can we go visit them?"

"Sure, but first we need to collect the eggs you're having for breakfast."

Curtis followed Moonbeam out the back door and into a little garden that she must take care of herself. It was similar to the one Senora Gonzalez had, but at the same time it was different. It was wilder and more overgrown. Moonbeam pointed out corn that she'd planted and a small tomato patch bearing green fruit. She showed him beans that she was growing and potatoes she'd planted from scratch. Curtis had only seen vegetables in the supermarket, so he took great interest in everything that Moonbeam showed him, wanting to touch everything.

Outside they entered another little house. Moonbeam signaled to Curtis to be quiet and pointed to the shelves where chickens had made nests. Upon spotting them the birds began squawking and some flew into the air. Moonbeam used that time to select four brown eggs from a few of the empty nests.

"What about the rest?" Curtis asked.

"They'll hatch into baby chickens."

Curtis began clapping his hands. "Goodie." The noise startled more chickens and they rose and flew directly at them.

"Time to visit the goats," Moonbeam said, grabbing his hand and racing out the door.

The baby goats were running around chasing their mother when he and Moonbeam approached.

"Do they have names yet?" Curtis asked as the animals stopped what they were doing and stared at him.

"I never got around to naming them," Moonbeam admitted, "Maybe you can think something up."

"I like the one with the white patch on his belly. He reminds me of my stuffed toy at home. I'll call him Starlight."

Moonbeam smiled. "That's a fine name. It matches my own. And what will you name the other?"

"Sunshine, just like we're having this morning."

"You're a funny little boy," Moonbeam said, this time laughing out loud. "Let's get you breakfast and then you can play with your new friends. I've got work to do."

Curtis sat down to a breakfast of scrambled eggs and bread. When he was done Moonlight told him it was okay to go out and play with Starlight and Sunshine but that he should be careful as sometimes the mother goat did bite. Curtis wondered how his father was doing and if he was looking for him. He also thought about his mother and wondered how he would get home.

All his worries were put temporarily aside as the goats greeted him noisily. Curtis chased them about, rolling around in the green grass as the baby goats nudged him with their mouths. Moonbeam had set up an easel under a shady tree. She kept an eye on him as she sketched and sang in a loud off-key voice. Moonbeam didn't seem to have a care in the world and she didn't shout at him. Curtis was beginning to like living with her but he knew he couldn't stay here forever. She wasn't his real mother and he needed to get home.

Chapter 15

"Yes, yes. That's him," Jude Martin said as Kristie spread out Curtis's pictures in front of the woman she'd agreed to meet at a restaurant.

It was a popular one right off the Southern State Parkway. This evening it was packed with the after-work crowd grabbing an early-bird dinner.

Jude Martin was not at all what Kristie expected. She was a tiny, nervous woman who spoke a mile a minute, and twisted her streaked blond hair as she spoke.

"I knew something was up from the moment that man left the park," Jude said vehemently. "I mean, what responsible father would up and leave a little boy alone in Mexico with people he didn't even know?"

"Earl just left Curtis alone?" Kristie cried, outraged. "He left my little boy in a park with strangers?"

"Yes, he did," Jude said, sucking down the Coke that she'd ordered while her son, Kevin, kicked his feet out in front of him and played with a handheld computer game. "My husband and I ended up taking Curtis back to our hotel with us. What else could we do?" Jude gesticulated with long red nails, making her point.

"Thank God you did," Kristie said. "Thank God you had the presence of mind to keep my child with you. I could kick myself for not getting the media involved before now. If I had, maybe Curtis would be home right now and not with my jackass of an ex-husband."

Kevin looked at her. "Uh-oh. You said a bad word."

"Sorry."

Jude patted Kristie's arm. "Don't blame yourself. The man came strutting through our hotel claiming his wallet was stolen. Henry paid for his cab and he promised to get our money back to us. Of course that never happened."

"That's pretty typical of Earl," Kristie said sourly.

Jude reached across the table and squeezed Kristie's hand. "My gut told me something was wrong, but Henry thought I was overreacting. You know men, when you tell them you're going on instinct, you're labeled a hysterical woman."

Kristie's attention turned to the little boy sitting across from his mother. "You played with my little boy, Curtis?" she asked.

"Ummm-hmmm. We're friends."

"And how was he? Did he seem happy to you?"

"Hmmm-ummm. He told me he missed his mother."

"Did he say where his mother was?"

Kristie stared at the child, waiting for him to answer. Every word he said was important and could lead to her son. She needed to listen, really listen to his response.

"Well, Kevin, did he?" Jude prompted when the boy didn't answer right off.

"Curtis said you were at home and that his dad had taken him on vacation to reward him because he was doing well at school."

What a liar her ex was. Kristie directed the next question to Jude. "How did Earl look to you? Did he seem focused, like someone you would trust with a child?"

Jude hesitated. "I didn't like his looks. He seemed dirty and agitated and kept looking around as if someone was after him."

"They probably were," Kristie muttered. She could only imagine that Earl's mind was probably on scoring his next hit and not on his son.

"I'm sorry. I didn't hear you," Jude said.

No point in repeating her words or airing her dirty laundry in public. Kristie had made the tough decision to get Earl out of her life. Maybe if she'd fought harder about not giving him visitation rights, none of this would have happened. But she'd felt that a child needed a father, even one as irresponsible as Earl.

"Henry thought I was being irrational and that I had little compassion for a man whose wallet was just stolen," Jude repeated.

"What hotel did you stay at?" Kristie asked, a plan beginning to formulate.

She and Zan needed a place to stay. The little she'd learned about Isle de Artistes indicated that hotels meeting American standards would be hard to find. If she stayed at the same hotel as the

Martins, the odds of finding an employee who'd actually seen her son would be greatly improved. Not that she doubted Jude Martin's version one bit.

"Our hotel was called Villa Rosa," Jude said, slurping her Coke loudly. "The Hilton it wasn't, but it was the best we could do."

Kristie wondered why the Martins had chosen Isle de Artistes to vacation on. She could picture the blonde in Cancun, Acapulco, or Puerto Vallarta, places that American tourists tended to frequent.

"Henry heard about the island from one of his golfing buddies," Jude supplied. "He said the American dollar went far there and my husband likes a good bargain."

As aggravated and upset as Kristie was, she couldn't help smiling. Jude had painted an interesting picture of her spouse. She gave Jude her cell number and signaled the waitress over. Jude stood and held out a hand to her son. "Come on, sweetie, let's go."

"Good-bye, Kevin," Kristie said, signing the credit card slip and leaving it on the table.

Kevin was out of his seat like a shot. "Can I have Curtis over for a play date when you find him?" He tugged on his mother's jeans. "Can I, Mom?"

"Of course you can. Say a prayer for Curtis tonight." Jude linked her fingers securely through her son's. "Good luck to you," she said, kissing Kristie's cheek.

"Thank you. I'll stay in touch."

Kristie walked with them to the parking lot. She tried her best not to cry as she watched mother and son get into their car. The brief encounter with

Jude Martin had made her realize how much she missed Curtis and how empty life was without him. No point in getting more upset than she was. Her sole mission now was to find her son.

"Fasten your seat belts and bring your seats to an upright position. We're landing in ten minutes," a male flight attendant said over the intercom. The remaining crew scurried through the aisles collecting plastic glasses and crumpled napkins.

Kristie was asleep, her head on Zan's shoulder. He loved watching her sleep. It had taken everything he had not to put his arms around her and hold her close. But this was no honeymoon. She'd told him about meeting with Jude Martin last evening and how the woman had recognized Curtis instantly once Kristie showed his picture.

Kristie had been optimistic, even upbeat, when she'd greeted him at the door. She'd been bubbling over with the news and confident that they would find Curtis on Isle de Artistes. Zan had had Miriam do research on the Internet. She'd found out that the island was only about twenty-two miles long and thirty miles wide. It was mountainous in some places and housed a combination of American expatriates and locals seeking to escape a hectic life.

Isle de Artistes had recently embraced tourism, as it needed foreign money to survive. The devalued peso made for a shaky economy, and the tourism board was working diligently to get more exposure for the island.

Kristie stirred next to Zan and sighed.

"Time to wake up, hon," he said, shaking her gently.

"Why? Are we there?"

"Soon."

She yawned and stretched and he smoothed her hair.

Bill Federicks was meeting them on the island. He'd departed for Isle de Artistes once Zan had filled him in on the police's suspicions. Bill, through his sources, had managed to confirm that Earl and Curtis had taken a flight to Cancun with an onward connection.

The plane's engine rumbled and one wing dipped. Zan stared down at an azure sea and at tiny white villas rising off the cliffs. It looked like paradise to him. At any other time he would have looked forward to this trip. The thought of lying on white sandy beaches and taking in the rays would have been exciting. But there wouldn't be much of that on this trip. They were here to find Curtis, not loll around.

Kristie clutched Zan's arm as they prepared for touchdown. "Oh, God, I'm so nervous," she said.

He patted her hand. "Relax."

She sank back into her seat and this time Zan did wrap an arm around her. He'd never in his wildest dreams think that he would enjoy being with someone like this, a woman who so obviously needed him. Inwardly Kristie was a nervous wreck.

"We have confirmed reservations at the Villa Rosa?" Kristie asked for what seemed the hundredth time.

"We do, two rooms. Bill's staying at a nearby B-and-B. He felt that if he stayed with a local he would have a better shot of getting more pertinent information."

"This entire trip must be costing a bundle," Kristie said, sighing.

Zan squeezed her shoulder. "It's a small price to pay if we get Curtis back."

"True."

He'd started referring to Curtis as if he were his son. Time to regroup. A child, girlfriend, or wife was not part of the plan. Not right now while he was still growing his business.

The plane touched down on the tiny runway and the few passengers on board clapped. Kristie and Zan made it through immigration, collected their bags, and went through customs.

On the street the taxi they hailed was more like a minivan. It whizzed them down a one-lane road and into a picturesque town.

The Villa Rosa was a sprawling hacienda shrouded in bougainvillea. Zan paid the driver and helped Kristie out. An aging bellhop took their luggage and they proceeded up several steps. Registration was a formality and then they were shown to adjoining rooms by an attractive hostess.

"How much time do you need to freshen up?" Zan asked.

Kristie glanced at her watch. "Maybe twenty minutes."

"You got it, babe. We'll meet in the lobby, have a quick bite, and then head out."

Kristie followed the hostess into her room and Zan waited until she'd shut the door. The luggage, he presumed, had already been sent up. For one brief moment he wished that he were sharing a room with Kristie. A hotel like this would be the perfect place to honeymoon. It was tiny and intimate and offered everything he needed.

Good Lord, what could he be thinking? It wasn't as if he was dating the woman. He'd kissed her once and only to comfort her. *Liar.* She wasn't the type he normally went for either, nor would she fit into his life, he reminded himself. Truth was it felt good having her depend on him and he was having the hardest time keeping his hands to himself. S*top it, Zan.*

Twenty minutes later, after a quick shower and change of clothes, Zan waited in the lobby. Kristie descended the winding staircase with her hair slicked back, looking awfully young in an ankle-length white linen dress with two slits on the sides. Why did this have to be a business trip?

"Let's get started," she said, joining him on the rattan couch.

"We'll talk to the employees and see if anyone remembers Earl and Curtis. Based on what the Martin woman said, there must have been quite the scene in the lobby."

"Bill might have already done that," Kristie responded, looking at him with those tawny eyes of hers. Zan crossed his legs so that she wouldn't see the effect she was having on him.

He began speaking quickly. Too quickly. "Look, even if Bill did speak with the employees, don't you think that Curtis's mother would have a better shot of finding out more information? You're an exceptionally good-looking woman, use every edge that you have."

Kristie blushed. She seemed thoroughly thrown by the compliment. "Okay," she said, getting up in a rush. "I'll start with the front desk. You speak with the concierge." She headed off in the direction of reception and Zan approached the bellhop's desk.

A pompous-looking man presided. He looked at Zan over half-moon glasses. "May I help you?"

Zan was tempted to slap down his business card but on second thought that might not be wise. Lawyers were often not well regarded.

"I'm trying to get in touch with friends that are staying on the island," Zan said, lowering his voice. "I thought they were here at the Villa Rosa but I can't seem to find them listed."

The puffed-up little man drew himself up to full height, five feet six, if that. He sniffed. "If your friends are not here at the Villa, then they must be at one of the two-star hotels or at one of the little inns."

"Hmmmm," Zan said. "That presents a problem. There must be many two-star hotels and twice as many inns."

"We are speaking of American people?"

"Yes, black American people."

The concierge pursed his lips. "We do not get many Negroes visiting. If any had been here I would have remembered. My memory is excellent." He tapped an index finger to his temple.

"Negro" is the word for black in Spanish. There was no racial slur intended. Zan buttoned his lip.

"Well, now, let's see. Last week a black man and a child were in the lobby. They were not guests here. I did not serve them."

"What did this man look like? Was he of average height and clean shaven? Did the little boy have a missing tooth?"

The concierge considered for a while and Zan slapped down two photos and began counting twenty-dollar bills. Maybe the sight of cash would prompt the man's memory.

"He was with two of our guests," the concierge said, memory returning.

"That would be the Martins," Zan supplied. "Friends of ours."

"Your friends paid the man's taxi fare. He'd lost his wallet, or so he said."

Zan slid several crisp twenty-dollar bills across the counter. "If you remember anything else at all, please feel free to ring my room. The name is McManus."

The concierge bowed. "It will be my pleasure. Jorge Sabotina knows the name of every guest."

"I bet," Zan said, turning away in time to see a visibly upset Kristie hurrying toward him.

"Curtis was here," she said when she was a foot or so away. "My little boy was here."

"Yes, I know," Zan said, placing an arm around Kristie's shoulder. "We'll get a bite to eat and decide the next step."

The meager breakfast they'd been served on the airplane left Zan hungry. His stomach rumbled and the altitude made him feel light-headed. Holding Kristie by the elbow he guided her across the lobby following signs written in both Spanish and English. They headed toward a poolside restaurant in a pretty outdoor area where more of the climbing bougainvillea prevailed.

A cute Mexican woman, dressed in the traditional garb of flowing skirt and gauzy peasant blouse, seated them. Zan ordered two Bloody Marys, figuring that Kristie needed something to soothe her nerves. He scrutinized the menu, then said, "What did you find out?"

She told him that a woman at the reception desk remembered Curtis, and Zan shared what the concierge had said.

"We can't just sit here," Kristie pleaded. "We need to do something."

"We will. As soon as we've eaten I'll call Bill."

Kristie had a difficult time ordering so Zan ordered them both tortilla soup and they shared arroz con pollo. Once he'd signaled for the check, Kristie was on her feet again.

"Let's go find Bill."

They were crossing the lobby and Zan had just gotten his cell phone out when Senor Sabotina intercepted them.

"I have news for you," he said, tapping a folded-up newspaper. "The man who came to our lobby was arrested."

"What?" Kristie looked as if she were about to faint.

Jorge Sabotina unfolded the paper and shoved it under Zan's nose. A sensational headline screamed at him: AMERICAN MAN ARRESTED ON CHARGES OF CO-CAINE POSSESSION.

The color photo beneath accompanied the blurb. Earl was flanked by two officers as they snapped handcuffs on him.

Zan silently handed Kristie the paper. She stared at it for a moment, the tears slowly sliding down her face. He opened his arms and she fell into them, laid her head on his chest, and began to sob.

Zan wanted to strangle Earl Leone.

Chapter 16

The rank odors nearly made Earl sick. He squatted on the floor of the filthy cell, too afraid to sit. He wished that he had something to dull his senses and make him forget the mess he was in. Daylight had brought with it a painful sobriety and shaky hands. Scenes from last night filtered through his memory like the trailers of a bad movie. How did he get himself into this mess?

The mostly Spanish inmates were in for an assortment of crimes: anything ranging from petty theft to prostitution. There were other drug dealers like him, jabbering away in a foreign language and taking sideways glances at him, the only black man there. Earl held his breath and tried not to inhale. He looked around at the piles of human excrement that had begun to solidify on the concrete floor.

He couldn't possibly raise bail if such a thing were even offered. The few dollars he'd had on him had been taken away. How was Curtis, a six-year-old, supposed to survive on the streets? It didn't make Earl feel good that he'd been a negligent parent. He screwed up royally with Kristie and there would be no forgiveness now.

"Cigarillo?" a man in his twenties mumbled to no one in particular. He approached Earl and made a gesture from hand to mouth. Earl knew enough Spanish to figure out he was begging for a cigarette.

Earl slowly rose, shaking his head. "No *cigarillo*. No smoke."

Not exactly true. He didn't smoke cigarettes, just other stuff.

The acrid stench of urine almost made him retch as a middle-aged man relieved himself in the corner. Earl swallowed the bile, knowing that retching would only add to the already foul odor. He gave in to the sense of hopelessness that shrouded him. No one knew where he was. He would be left to rot in this Mexican jail. He had to do something.

"I want a public defender," Earl shouted, rattling the bars that separated him from freedom. "I demand the phone call that I'm owed."

The racket he put up sent two policemen scurrying. They shouted something in Spanish and banged their sticks against the bars. A bloated red-faced cop entered and took charge. He spoke English.

"You have no rights," he said, his spittle flecking across Earl's cheeks.

"I want a lawyer," Earl repeated. "At the very least someone from the American embassy needs to know I'm here."

"No hablo inglés," the red-faced man said, although he had managed quite well up until now.

Earl rattled the bars again. "Look, find me some-one who does speak English then."

His request was ignored as the policemen con-ferred. They shouted something at him in Spanish, then disappeared.

Earl stared at his shaking hands and thought about how much he needed a joint. He needed something that would dull his senses and help ease the pain, something that would make him for-get about this Hades called a Mexican jail.

"I've been trying to reach that friend of yours but so far no answer," Ed said, stuffing pasta into his mouth.

"Which friend would that be?" Lizette asked, pre-tending she didn't know. She paused with her fork midway to her mouth.

"Kristie, of course."

She'd invited Ed for dinner and was beginning to regret it. So far he'd been preoccupied and she'd begun to wonder why he'd come.

Ed eyed her over his fork. "When was the last time you two spoke?"

"She's out of town," Lizette reluctantly answered.

The cutlery clattered as Ed set it down. "Phillips's son is missing and she's gadding about?"

"Kristie's not gadding about as you so sarcasti-cally put it. She's a responsible parent and took a leave of absence. She's on her way to Mexico right now."

"And you didn't mention this before," Ed said, shoving his chair back and getting out his cell phone.

Lizette gaped at his rudeness. The meal that she'd rushed home to prepare would get cold and all because Ed had some type of burr up his ass. He was obsessed with Kristie.

"Banks is nowhere to be found," Ed said, shutting the phone down, and slamming into his seat.

He began shoveling down pasta just like before. Lizette had just about enough of him.

"Since when does Kristie have to check in with you? Is she under suspicion for kidnapping her own son? The woman did what any heartbroken mother would do. She's flying to Isle de Artistes to look for the child herself."

"She's on a wild-goose chase. These types of situations are better left to the police."

"Law enforcement hasn't done squat for her so far. Ryan Velox is the one who reached out to help her."

Ed's jaw muscles worked. Lizette guessed she'd pushed his hot buttons. Well, he'd pushed hers too.

"Your friend is flying to Isle de Artistes alone?" Ed's eyebrows shot to the ceiling.

"No, Zan's with her."

"The attorney?"

"Yes."

Lizette had fallen into Ed's trap, offered too much information. He sat back, smiling at her. "Most lawyers can't just drop everything and fly off with clients."

"Zan McManus just did."

"Gotta be something going on with those two."

Lizette kept her mouth closed; expressing that same sentiment would be disloyal. Besides, Kristie could certainly do worse than Zan McManus. He was every woman's dream.

She tried changing the topic. "So how was your day?"

"The usual." Ed finished his pasta with relish and pushed his plate away. "You're some cook."

"Thank you." Lizette got up and began gathering plates.

Ed surprised her by helping. "What now?" he asked when the last dish was placed in the dishwasher.

"You want coffee and dessert?"

"I want you," he said, taking her hand and leading her into the bedroom.

They stopped in front of the floor-length mirror and his hands covered both breasts, stroking and titillating the nipples. "You've got the most beautiful boobs."

"Yeah, right."

Deep down she felt that Ed's interest in her might be purely sexual but she was determined to go with the flow. While he might be using her to get information about Kristie, she was also using him and he'd made no bones about finding her attractive.

Ed began to stroke her all over. He popped the buttons of her blouse and pushed the fabric off her shoulders. She managed to peek into the mirror and all her senses heightened as she saw his long lean body and thrusting manhood rubbing against her.

Lizette noticed her flushed face and the way her nipples had come to full attention under Ed's ministrations. He lowered his mouth to tug on a nipple and his fingers dove into her crotch, weaving through the coarse hairs. She tugged on Ed's belt buckle.

"Oh, baby, we should get out of these confining clothes," he said, moving away and sliding out of his jeans.

Naked, they looked into the mirror. "You've got some figure," Ed said, patting her rump.

Lizette had never thought of her body as anything special. She was a big girl and in another era would be considered Rubenesque. But Ed's admiring looks made her feel as if she were the most gorgeous woman on earth and there was something to be said for that.

She stood on tiptoe, wrapped her arms around his neck, and kissed him. Ed kissed her back, letting his tongue explore and tease, making promises that he was quite capable of delivering.

"Oh, baby," he said, squeezing her butt. "You smell so good. You taste so good. You feel so good."

Lizette suspected these were the lines he used on all women. She couldn't help being cautious; men like Ed didn't normally go for her. Even so, she held his shaft in one hand and squeezed gently. Ed immediately began to moan. He nipped on her neck and shoulders before his hands moved down to stroke her stomach and delve into the apex at her thighs.

Lizette forgot about his bizarre fascination with Kristie or the possibility that she was being used. Ed swung her up, holding her over his head. He kissed her stomach and drove her wild. She wanted him inside her. Ed set her down and gently lowered her to the floor. One knee parted her thighs as he slid a condom on.

Ed was crooning words she barely understood and didn't want to believe. His lips tugged at her earlobes before his tongue settled in the hollow at her throat. Lizette bucked against him, wanting even more. Ed entered her and let the friction build. He thrusted in and out of her until she was wild. Then he turned her on her side and entered her from the rear, filling her up until she thought she would burst.

Lizette smelled his heat and felt his touch and heard noises coming from the back of his throat. The world around her ebbed and flowed. She'd reached a point of no return. She screamed his name and felt her blood roar.

"Give me that," Kristie said, snatching the newspaper article from the concierge's hand. She gazed at the photo of Earl being led away in handcuffs, unable to believe that at one time this man had been her husband.

A tiny cry escaped her lips as she read the details of his arrest. How could he do this? How could he place her child in danger and all because he had no willpower? He was an addict. She'd been married to an addict. But what concerned her even more was that there was no mention of Curtis. She had to find her child. She didn't want him wandering the streets alone.

Zan read over her shoulder. He tossed the question out to Sabotina. "Where is this jail?"

The concierge spoke to a bellhop in rapid Spanish, then turned back to them to explain. "It's at least a forty-minute trip through rugged terrain. The jail is located in an isolated part of the island. You might want to call and find out when visiting hours are."

"Do you mind if we keep this newspaper?" Kristie asked.

"Not at all, it is my pleasure to give it to you."

Sabotina hurried off to greet other guests getting out of taxis.

"Are you okay?" Zan asked, placing a comforting arm around her shoulders.

"I guess I'm still numb. It's slowly sinking in that my ex has been arrested on drug-related charges and no one knows where Curtis is."

Zan hugged her to him. "You know what I think?" Kristie didn't answer. "I think we should find Bill, then go out and look for Curtis."

"Yes, let's."

They made their way outside and Zan, with the aid of a bellhop, got them a taxi. Pulling out a pocket organizer, he stared at it, then rattled off an address in fluent Spanish.

Kristie gazed out at the scenery as it whizzed by. She saw the pretty pastel-colored buildings and blooming flowers spilling from pots. She heard the vendors hawking their wares and noticed the easels on which artists painted caricatures of tourists.

In a remote part of her brain it registered that this would be the perfect spot for an intimate little vacation, but she wasn't here for a vacation. Her mission was to find Curtis. The man who sat beside her nudged her thigh making her blood pump, but she ignored it. Zan was her attorney, not her lover, though it was increasingly more difficult to remember that. In idle moments she'd found herself daydreaming about what it would be like to be with him.

Kristie had never dated someone like Zan, polished, successful, and too handsome for his own good. Earl had struggled all his life and had never really held down a job. He'd never really wined and dined her either. But though he'd been charming and she'd fallen into the relationship because it was easy, she'd never felt safe with him. Kristie had always been waiting for the next shoe to drop, and it did, more often than she cared to admit.

"You're awfully quiet," Zan said, breaking into her musings.

"I have a lot on my mind. All I can think about is Curtis. Where could that child possibly have spent the night?"

Kristie felt guilty for lying to Zan. She had been thinking about their kiss with vivid awareness. Her toes had tingled and her heart still raced but she would never tell him that.

The taxi stopped in front of a modest-looking house.

"This is where Bill's staying," he explained, helping her out of the cab and peeling some bills from his wallet.

The driver pocketed the money and took off in a cloud of smoke. They started up a pathway and climbed three crumbling steps. Zan banged on the door and they heard footsteps approach.

"*Hola,*" the young woman who answered greeted them. "You are American, no? You are looking for a room?"

"Yes, we are American. And no, we are not looking for a room. We are here to see Bill Federicks."

The woman waved them inside. "*Por favor,* have a seat," she said, gesturing toward an overstuffed couch. "Let me knock on his bedroom door and see if he answers."

As they sat waiting, Kristie spotted an older woman in the kitchen stirring a pot that smelled heavenly.

Bill, an older man with salt-and-pepper hair, joined them and Zan made introductions.

"Are you comfortable here?" Zan asked Bill when the young woman was out of earshot. He eyed the shabby furniture and stained walls, wrinkling his nose.

"I'm quite comfortable, thank you. Senora Gonzalez, the proprietor, speaks very little English. Her daughter, Esperanza, whom you just met, is the one conversant in English. To tell you the truth I like it that way."

Zan halted the man's ramblings. "What have you found out?"

"It may be pure coincidence but it seems that Earl and Curtis stayed here."

"My little boy was here?" Kristie repeated, looking around the humble home and feeling an immediate affinity for the place where her child had resided. "I'd like to speak with Esperanza. Do you think that would be possible?"

"Esperanza," Bill called. "Please come out here."

The young woman returned with an anxious expression on her face. "Senor, what is it?"

"Ms. Phillips is Curtis's mother. She would like to ask you some questions about him."

"Senora Phillips is the *madre?* Mr. Leone said his wife was dead."

"Mr. Leone lied. I'm healthy and alive and I've come for my son," Kristie practically spat out.

"I don't understand."

"Mr. Leone abducted Curtis."

Esperanza scrunched up her nose. "Abduct? What does that mean?"

"It means he took him out of the country illegally without his mother's permission," Zan explained.

"Curtis is a nice boy. He loved our Pobrecito. When he ran away he took him with him."

"Where could Curtis have gone to?" Kristie asked. "Did he have friends?"

Esperanza scrunched up her nose again. "I don't know. I don't think so. Curtis, I think, wanted to get away from his father. He was, what do you say, mean."

Kristie fisted her hands. She wanted to punch something. "Earl hurt my child?"

"He hit him when he drank. My mother and I did not want to interfere. Mr. Leone paid his rent on time and we needed the money."

A woofing came from some place in the back of the house. A skinny mongrel stood in the doorway eyeing them warily.

"I thought Curtis took your dog with him," Zan said.

"Yes, he did, but Pobrecito found his way back home. This morning we heard about Mr. Leone's arrest. What a terrible thing. To think he sold drugs and he lived here."

"I want to find my child," Kristie said crisply and clearly. She'd had enough of the banter.

"I've already contacted the authorities," Bill assured her.

"You went to the airport? What if my son is trying to get home?"

"I haven't done that."

"Then get to it," Zan barked. "Start talking to people on the streets, anyone who might have seen Curtis. We need to split up. Get the map and we'll decide what streets we'll take. We'll meet back here within the hour and discuss our findings."

Zan was very much in charge as they hunkered down over the crumpled map that Bill spread on the floor. His index finger swept up and down several streets closely located to the house.

"Ms. Phillips, if I may make a recommendation, why don't you stick to the main thoroughfare?" Bill said. "Zan and I can do the side streets in the raunchier parts of town."

"Good idea," Zan said, leading them out. "Kristie, I want you to be careful. If for any reason you feel uncomfortable you are to return to this house immediately. Do we understand each other?"

"But of course."

Kristie liked Zan's bossiness because it made her feel special and cared for. Men didn't come much better than him. However, she feared she was beginning to fall in love with him and that was not necessarily a good thing.

Chapter 17

Curtis pressed a nose to the window, fascinated by the arrival of the mailman, who looked like no other mailman he'd seen before. He leapt out of a pickup truck and strode up the walkway. Dressed in jeans and a big hat, he reminded Curtis of the cowboys he'd seen on TV.

He banged on Moonbeam's front door and her face lit up. She rushed to answer it.

"Hey, Jose. Want some of my homemade brew?" she greeted, letting the tall thin man with the bushy mustache in.

"Course I do. Your brew's the best. Who's the little boy?" he asked, spotting Curtis.

"A child I found wandering around town." Moonbeam toddled out to the backyard and returned with a pitcher. "Took this out of the stream, helps keep it cold," she said, pouring their drinks. "I have a favor I need."

"Shoot. Anything for you." Jose's voice didn't sound American. There was a strange sound to it.

"I need you to take a note into town for me. Someone's gotta be looking for this child." Moonbeam darted a look at Curtis, then lowered her voice. Curtis could still hear her clearly. "His mother's gotta be looking for him. She may still be in the United States."

"Where do I drop off this note?"

"At the U.S. embassy. If he's missing, they'll know what to do."

"Isn't there a father?"

Moonbeam shrugged. "He may be a problem."

Jose cocked his head to the side. "I wonder if he's the guy in the newspaper."

"What guy in the newspaper?"

"I'll be right back," Jose said, disappearing out the front door and returning a few minutes later with a paper folded under his arm.

Curtis was dying to see what was in the paper. Instead he watched Moonbeam and Jose huddle over it.

"Well, I'll be damned," Moonbeam said after a while. She called Curtis over and pointed to a photo of his dad surrounded by two other men. "Curtis, is that your father?"

"Yes," he said, mad at himself because his voice squeaked. His dad did not look happy and the men with him looked even unhappier.

"Dumb ass," Jose said, draining his glass. "He brings his little boy to Mexico and gets involved in something like this."

"Even more reason to take my note to the embassy," Moonbeam said, grabbing a pad and scribbling on it. Curtis wished he could see what she was writing. She folded the paper and handed it to Jose. "I don't have an envelope."

He pocketed the note, kissed Moonbeam on the lips, and said, "Too bad you have company, babe. I gotta get going."

"Hurry back soon," Moonbeam said, wrapping her arms around his waist and pressing her body against him.

Yuk, Curtis thought. Why did adults like to kiss? The girls at school were always trying to kiss him.

"Till tomorrow, babe. See you then, champ." Jose pinched his cheek and walked toward the front door.

Curtis heard the truck start up and the wheels spin against the gravel as he drove off.

"I hope my note does some good," Moonbeam said, picking up a paintbrush she'd left on the kitchen counter and heading for the back door. "Bet you'll be glad to see your mother."

Curtis didn't really know what she was talking about but it sounded as if Moonbeam was trying to help him get home and he liked that. He wanted to sleep in his own bed and he missed his friends. He even missed school. Much as he liked Moonbeam, it was time to go home.

Kristie slid into the passenger side of the rented Jeep. Bill was already ensconced in the back. Yesterday's efforts had not yielded much but enough to deduce that Curtis was trying to make his way home. Kristie had questioned every vendor and store owner on Main Street and described her boy. She'd passed out fliers with Curtis's picture, and several people had admitted seeing him.

Eventually she'd come to Mr. Santiago's store. The man had beamed from ear to ear when he'd spotted the photo of Curtis. He'd been more than willing to talk. Kristie had questioned him and learned that her little boy had liked his store and had even tried calling her from there.

Bill and Zan had also learned that there had been sightings of Curtis at the bus depot. Several vendors had admitted to seeing him with a dog but no one seemed to know exactly where he was heading.

They'd decided to take the forty-minute drive to the jail where Earl was being detained. It really wasn't something Kristie wanted to do. She wasn't ready to see Earl. She was furious at him for taking Curtis away and for getting himself locked up in a Mexican jail.

"You okay?" Zan asked, patting her leg.

"Yes, I suppose." Kristie was afraid to voice what she was really feeling. She was afraid to admit how angry she was and how nervous she was about seeing Earl again. In so many ways she'd been his protector, his enabler. Her own thoughts frightened her. She'd wanted to murder Earl. What could he have been thinking of, selling dope and getting himself arrested?

Zan consulted a map and put the Jeep into gear. They were on their way. Ten minutes later they'd left the small village and entered a more rural setting. They bounced their way down the dirty gravel roads toward the jail. Kristie stared out the window at the pretty countryside as it went by, not really registering anything. Bill had called the jail earlier, confirming that Earl was there. But no one seemed able to tell them if there were visiting hours so they'd decided to take the drive. It was their only chance of talking to Earl.

Zan braked as a cow crossed the street. Kristie's body collided with his. She was painfully aware of the man seated next to her. He smelled of soap and a masculine cologne she couldn't put a name to. He smelled like Zan, unique and very tempting.

"I tried to find out if we could bail Earl out," Bill said from the backseat. "No one could tell me a thing."

"As far as I'm concerned he can rot in hell," Kristie said, breaking her silence. "I'm just interested in getting my child back."

"And you will," Zan said confidently.

"How can you be sure? No one has seen Curtis in almost two days. He could have been kidnapped. He might even be dead." Her voice broke.

Zan patted her leg. "Curtis is fine." He made a quick right and bounced down another road. "Another five minutes and we'll be there."

Kristie spotted the grim gray building looming up against a blue sky. The walls surrounding it had rolls of barbwire on top. A tower in the center was manned by two guards whose guns were pointed directly at them. Why was she here? How would this all end?

Two prison guards flagged them down and demanded something in Spanish. Zan seemed to understand what they were saying.

"Get out your identification. Show them your passport."

Kristie dug through her bag and handed her passport over. After the men were done scrutinizing the documents they handed them back. One of them waved them through.

"That was easy," Bill said, as huge wrought-iron

gates opened and they drove in. There were more stops on the way, more scrutiny of their passports. They parked next to a handful of battered vehicles. Kristie climbed out of the Jeep before Zan could come around to the passenger side.

"What's the plan?" she asked.

"We go inside."

He took her hand while Bill loped ahead.

"I've never been in a prison before," Kristie admitted. "I'm scared."

"No need to be. I won't let anything bad happen to you."

Inside, a grim-faced woman dressed in a drab khaki uniform greeted them. She scrutinized their identification and demanded something in Spanish.

"*Habla inglés?*" Zan asked.

"*Un poquito, pero solamente un poquito.*"

This was going to be fun. No one spoke English.

Zan answered in Spanish, rattling off Earl's name. He produced a photo and the woman scanned it. She shouted for someone and two men dressed in the same khaki garb came out of a back room. They looked at Earl's picture but didn't comment before disappearing again.

Fifteen minutes elapsed before another man came out of the back office. He gestured to them to follow him and they walked down a long corridor.

There were guttural noises and a foul smell before Kristie spotted the cell. It looked more like a pen where animals were kept, and in fact it was simply a cage where human beings were held. The captured inside had assumed the stance of the hunted, eyeing the outside world warily, conditioned to not trusting.

Thirty or forty inmates were crammed together in a space that realistically should have held half that many. There was no visible sign of a lavatory or a place where people could clean up. There was also no one fitting Earl's description in clear view.

Zan cleared his throat and in rapid Spanish said, *"Donde es Senor Leone?"*

The guard pointed his finger at the cage and all four moved closer. Kristie had never seen such an appalling sight: men herded into a tight unsanitary area. She wanted to pinch her nostrils until she could no longer smell. She fought to ease the nausea that she wanted to expel. Zan held tightly to her elbow and she leaned on him, welcoming his support. *Good Lord, let this be over with soon.*

The inmates began to stir, staring at the visitors that were different from the relatives that visited. Kristie scanned the pen again, hoping to see Earl. She made eye contact with a lean young man that was cadaverous in appearance.

He pushed a claw through one of the openings and bellowed at her. *"Cigarillo?"*

Bill shook a cigarette free from a pack in his breast pocket. Kristie didn't know he smoked. He looked to the guard for approval.

"Can I give him a butt?"

The guard nodded. Bill handed the man the entire pack.

"Gracias," he said, doing a good imitation of a genuflection and lighting up. Others came toward the bars, hands outstretched, jabbering words in their native language that made no sense to Kristie. As the sea parted, Kristie spotted Earl in a crouched

position in a far corner. He seemed uninterested
in what was going on.

"There he is," she whispered to Zan.

Zan maintained a tight grip on her elbow.
"Where?"

"He's wearing a blue T-shirt."

Earl's gaze locked with Kristie's. She couldn't
imagine how she'd ever lived with the man, or allowed him to make love to her.

Zan began waving Earl over. "I'm an attorney,"
he shouted over the chattering, yelling inmates. "I'd
like to help you."

He had to have lost his mind. Helping Earl was
the last thing any of them should do. As far as she
was concerned Earl could rot in jail, he'd get what
he deserved.

Kristie watched Earl unfurl his once powerful
body. He'd lost weight and was unshaven and unkempt. He debated whether he should move forward or remain in the space he had carved out for
himself. It seemed to take him forever to decide.

"You're in Mexico, moron," Zan shouted. "You
have no rights. We're your best shot. Better make
the best of the few minutes that we're here."

Zan must have gotten through to him, because
Earl made his way around the mass of human bodies and up to the front. Seeing him up close served
to put Kristie's teeth on edge.

"Where's my son?" she demanded.

"I don't know. He took off. Sorry."

She wanted to strangle him.

"Sorry isn't good enough," she said, getting into
his face. "You stole my child and brought him here,
now you lost him."

"He's my child too."

"Bastard."

Zan squeezed her arm lightly, hoping to calm her down.

Kristie was not to be calmed. "A six-year-old's wandering around frightened, that's if he's still alive. I've had to leave my job and fly here and all because you can't be trusted."

"I'm just as worried as you," Earl said, his eyes darting right, then left.

"So you say. Has Curtis made friends here? Does he have people that he visits?"

Earl splayed his palms defensively. "Mrs. Gonzales, the woman I rented a room from, took good care of Curtis. Usually I left him with her."

"Didn't work the last time, did it? He ran away from her and took her dog with him."

"How do you know?"

"I've already been to the Gonzaleses'. You don't think I would leave any stone unturned."

Kristie wanted to hurl herself against the bars, reach through them, and strangle Earl. She was frustrated and tired and wanted her boy. Zan, through some means of silent communication, released her arm. Bill took the other. He moved her away, hoping she would calm down.

Zan was now talking to Earl.

"Listen up, man," he said, "and listen up good." Kristie had never heard Zan resort to street vernacular. His index finger punctuated the air. "You're in a mess. I can try to get you out, but that requires my time and money. Bill, my buddy, is going to ask you questions. Answer them truthfully or we'll leave your butt to rot right here."

Go, Zan, Kristie wanted to say as he moved to her side and let Bill take over. From a distance Kristie smelled Earl's fear. She couldn't hear what the detective was saying and she couldn't make out Earl's mumbled answers, but she could tell that her ex was truly scared. Hopefully, if and when she found her son, Earl would have learned a valuable lesson. Maybe he would even straighten out his life.

The guard who'd accompanied them tapped his watch, indicating time was up. Kristie couldn't wait to breathe fresh air and hear what Zan and Bill had to say.

"We've got to go," Zan said, gesturing to Bill.

"You can't leave me here," Earl screamed, spittle settling at the corners of his mouth.

Zan's response was brutal. "Why not? We owe you nothing."

"These conditions are inhumane. You're violating my rights. "

"You have no rights," Zan said, preparing to walk away. "You're a drug dealer."

"What about bail? Did you ask about that? What about getting me out of here?"

"What about bail?" Zan shouted back.

"Is there such a thing as bail?" Bill asked the prison guard loud enough for Earl to hear.

"Bail?" The man shrugged. "Not sure I understand."

Kristie heard Earl whimpering, such a big man.

Zan removed his wallet from a back pocket and slowly began counting out notes. He handed a wad to Bill.

At the sight of money the inmates went wild. They began whooping and hollering while Earl continued to scream at the top of his lungs.

Turning their backs on the pitiful group, they returned to the front office.

"What can we do to get Mr. Leone out?" Bill asked the guard that had accompanied them.

"He committed a crime and must go to trial," the man responded.

"Understood. What date has been set up?"

"No date yet. It all depends."

"Depends on what?"

Bill, visibly irritated, slapped a couple hundred dollars down on a desk. "Will this help?"

"Maybe. We are fair people and do not want an international incident. I'll be right back." He disappeared into the tiny back room.

Kristie began to panic. If Earl were freed he would be forced to ride in the same vehicle as them. She didn't want him anywhere close.

Zan hugged her to him as if sensing her thoughts. "I won't let Earl hurt you, Kristie."

While his promise reassured her, all she wanted was to escape this horrible place and find her son.

The guard returned with another man and said to them, "We will let Mr. Leone go if you pay our government ten thousand American dollars. You will then take him directly to the airport and he will not return. *Comprende?*"

"Ten thousand dollars," Bill challenged. "That's ridiculous. He was caught with less than two grams of cocaine. We're not talking about a kilo."

"I consider this entrapment," Zan said. "Didn't you say you didn't want an international incident? Undoubtedly this will become one."

"That's our deal. Take it or leave it," the new guard said and turned on his heel.

Zan motioned to Bill, who followed him to the exit. He called over his shoulder, "No deal."

"Seven thousand," the prison guard countered. "That's our best offer."

"Five thousand and we can talk. Call me at the Villa Rosa and we'll get the deal done."

Kristie had to admire Zan's skills at negotiation as she emerged into a world that smelled sweeter than she remembered. She wanted to sink to her knees and kiss the dirt below. What she had just gone through was a nightmare. It equated to being in the bowels of hell. And hell wasn't a place she wanted to be. She'd experienced it already married to Earl Leone.

Chapter 18

"The FBI's been in touch with the authorities on Isle de Artistes," Ed said to Lizette.

She clutched the receiver, daring to hope. "Since when are the police and FBI friends?"

Ed's deep voice came through the earpiece, suggestive and sexy. "We collaborate on cases. We do what we have to do."

Lizette hated playing guessing games and wished that Ed would get to the point. One of the things she'd learned in their brief acquaintanceship was that there was no point in pushing him.

"What exactly has the FBI found out?" Lizette finally asked.

She'd been at home folding laundry when Ed called. Waiting, she continued the mindless business of lining up seams and tucking the warm clothing into neat little squares.

"Earl Leone has been arrested."

"What?" Lizette paused midtask. "What about Curtis?"

"Don't know. The guy was caught dealing. Someone might have set him up."

"That bastard." There was an ominous silence on the other end. "You mean to tell me that child is in a strange country all on his own?"

"No one seems to know where the boy is," Ed said.

Lizette's mind immediately turned to Kristie. "I've got to call Kristie. She must be frantic with worry. It's a good thing she has Zan with her."

"Is it?"

Ed obviously didn't care for Zan. He'd made that clear.

"So what's the plan?" Lizette asked.

"We're going to try to have Earl Leone extradited."

"To hell with Earl," Lizette snapped. "I'm more interested in what you guys are doing about finding Curtis."

"The Mexican police are on alert. We have an all points bulletin out for the boy. The FBI's on the island. Something will turn up. I'd like to see you, babe."

"I'm catching up on some chores. I'm folding my laundry," Lizette said, not wanting to make it easy for him.

"Stop folding. Let's have a drink. I know just the place in your neighborhood. I'll pick you up in half an hour."

"Can't do."

"Wear something pretty," Ed said, hanging up.

Lizette sighed. She'd already known her protests would fall on deaf ears. A half hour would give her time to shower and dress and yes, the laundry could

wait. She wanted to see Ed. She'd wear something
that would leave him drooling. The evening would
undoubtedly end with them in bed.

"Sure you won't join us for dinner?" Zan asked
as Bill climbed out of the Jeep and began heading
toward the boardinghouse's door.

"Thanks but I have several calls to make. I'm
hoping that someone will answer at the U.S. embassy."

"At this late hour?" Zan asked, frowning.

"You never know."

Bill was the expert.

"Well, if you change your mind, you know where
to reach me," Zan said, tapping his cell phone.

"Will do."

Bill stopped briefly to wave them off. He mounted
the three little steps that led to Mrs. Gonzalez's front
door. They'd spent the rest of the day patrolling
the streets looking for Curtis and asking questions
of anyone they encountered.

Zan waited until he was inside before putting
the vehicle in gear. "We'll go back to the hotel and
take a quick shower," he said to Kristie. "I'm starving. Maybe our friend Sabotina can recommend a
nice local restaurant."

Kristie hadn't realized until then just how hungry
she was. She hadn't eaten since forever, it seemed,
and now it was dark. There was little that could be
accomplished until tomorrow.

Zan pulled up to the entrance of their hotel and
Kristie got out of the vehicle while Zan went to
park.

"Meet you in the lobby in half an hour," he said, zooming off.

She was emotionally drained from her encounter with Earl. The thought of staying in her room with crazy thoughts crowding her head was depressing. Somewhere out there a six-year-old must be trying desperately to get home. She couldn't think of Curtis. Wouldn't. It would just make her cry.

Kristie took a lukewarm shower, then stood in front of the closet debating what to wear. This wasn't exactly a date but she wanted to look nice, and the temperature dictated that she wear something cool. After a while she settled on a baby-blue sundress with a wide skirt and tiny spaghetti straps. She added silver jewelry and slipped on flat beige sandals. In case the restaurant had air-conditioning, she added a wrap.

The humidity outside had made her hair curl. No amount of washing, shampooing, or blow-drying would straighten it out. She squirted mousse onto her palm and ran her fingers through the short haircut that was designed to withstand almost any situation.

After grabbing her purse, she started down the stairs. Zan was loping down the steps in front of her. He'd changed into chinos and a black shirt and he'd rolled his sleeves up. The view from the back had Kristie salivating. Such broad shoulders. Such nice buns.

Zan must have sensed Kristie behind him because he turned and threw her a dazzling smile. Kristie's stomach flip-flopped and the ocean roared in her ears. She smiled back.

"Nice outfit," Zan said as his eyes traveled the length of her.

Kristie's body heated up as she basked in his admiration. She was beginning to feel like a woman again.

"You don't look too shabby yourself," she said, noting the silver stud in his ear and the chain that circled his neck. The metal reflected off his cinnamon skin and he seemed totally relaxed.

"Where are we going?" Kristie asked.

"Close by. We have an early start tomorrow."

Zan stopped at the concierge's desk where a woman dressed in traditional garb replaced Mr. Sabotina.

"You make a nice couple," the woman said, smiling at them.

Zan acknowledged the compliment with a nod. Kristie wondered if they did.

"Is there a place within walking distance that you'd recommend for dinner?" Zan asked.

The woman didn't even consult her book.

"I know just the thing," she said. "It's small but the food is good and it is, how you say, romantic." She gave them directions.

After Zan tipped her they set off walking up a tree-lined street with lanterns hanging off the boughs. Five minutes later they arrived at the restaurant, a cute little place that looked like it might once have been a house. Tiny bistro tables were scattered on a small patio and a strolling guitarist serenaded patrons of every age.

The proprietor, a middle-aged man, greeted them. *"Hola, bienvenido."* He turned them over to a hostess.

"Would you prefer to sit inside or out?" she asked.

Zan looked to Kristie. "The choice is yours, hon."

"Outside please."

"You heard the lady," Zan said, taking Kristie's arm and following the hostess to a table positioned directly in front of a tinkling fountain.

Zan ordered them red wine and while they waited they perused the menu, trying to decide on several tempting appetizers.

"I wonder where Curtis is tonight," Kristie said, putting voice to her fears. "He could be wandering the streets or he might have fallen prey to some awful predator."

"Don't even think of it." Zan's fingers circled Kristie's wrist. "Curtis is fine. I feel it. Please try to relax and enjoy our time together."

Kristie hoped that, hungry as she was, she would at least be able to eat the food that other patrons seemed to be eating with such relish.

They placed their appetizer orders: shrimp for Zan and strips of yucca with a dipping sauce for Kristie.

While they waited a guitarist serenaded a young couple that stared into each other's eyes while taking long, slow sips of wine. After a while the musician moved on. He stopped at their table.

"Do you have a special request that I might play?" he asked in perfect English.

He'd obviously mistaken them for lovers. Kristie was about to tell him not to waste his time when Zan spoke up.

"You choose something," he said to the musician.

Startled, Kristie looked at Zan. He winked at her. Her stomach did a somersault and she put it down to hunger. The guitarist began strumming softly and she turned her attention to him.

"I will play something very special for you. You are in love, yes?"

If he only knew. The ballad was old and something played frequently on the radio but she couldn't put a name to it. Zan held her hand through the entire song. He tipped the musician and the man moved on.

Zan ordered another bottle of wine and Kristie slowly began to relax.

"You don't ever talk about your childhood," Kristie said, wanting to know. It seemed like a long time ago since he'd mentioned he'd been placed in the foster care system.

"I still find it somewhat painful," Zan admitted.

Kristie reached a hand across the table and twined her fingers through Zan's hand that was drumming a beat on the wooden surface. "Talk to me."

And he began to talk, telling her how he felt about his parents abandoning him, and about being placed in overcrowded homes where the caregivers really didn't give a damn. Zan spoke of the relief he'd felt when the McManuses had come to the rescue and adopted him, then of the desolation and abandonment he'd felt when they later died in a car accident. He spoke with fondness about the adoptive grandparents who'd raised him.

"You've had a hard time of it," Kristie said, squeezing his hand.

"No harder than you have. You've alluded to a violent ex-husband, you've gone through a painful divorce, and now here you are searching for a child that's missing."

"That may be so, but didn't you also mention reuniting with your real mother several years later? What was that like?"

For a moment she thought he wasn't going to answer. His hand had gone limp in hers.

"Difficult. Very difficult," Zan said after a while. "Thanks to the Internet I was finally able to locate my mother years later, but she was in a bad way. She'd contracted the HIV virus and was close to death."

"Was she happy to see you?"

"I guess she was. Happy, and ashamed that she'd so easily given me up. My mother, Daphne, explained that she'd been an abused woman, totally dominated by my father and afraid to challenge him. He'd abducted me and used me as leverage to get her back. Rather than trying to find me, she decided it was better to walk away. She opted for self-preservation rather than being united with her son."

"God, that must have been so difficult for her," Kristie said, her eyes brimming.

"I suppose it was. But even as an adult I had a hard time with it. I couldn't imagine ever walking away from my flesh and blood. But she did have her reasons and I supposed they were good ones."

"What about your father?"

"What about him? He's dead to me."

Kristie remained silent. Her troubles seemed nothing in comparison to what Zan had been through. But he'd survived. Thrived. And was now successful. He'd been able to move on. He was an amazing man.

They ate a tasty meal and passed on dessert. Noticing the lateness of the hour, Kristie suggested they go home. The wine had produced a numbing effect and she was glad to have Zan's steadying arm around her waist. She laid her head on his shoulder and wished that they had come to the island under different circumstances. The lobby was de-

serted when they entered and they headed upstairs.

Zan slowed in front of her room. She peeled
herself off of him.

"It was a wonderful night. Thank you," Zan said.
"We shouldn't have had that second bottle of wine.
It makes me not want to leave you." He took her
key from her and opened the door.

Zan's hand cupped her chin and he bent over
to kiss her. The ceiling above began to rotate in
circles. Kristie placed a stilling hand on his chest,
hoping to get her equilibrium back. She didn't
want the evening to end; she also didn't want to
be alone, with crazy, frightening thoughts crowding in. What would she do if Curtis were never
found? She wasn't ever going to give up like Zan's
mother had.

Her fears must have been silently communicated.

"I'm coming in," Zan said, unlocking the door.

"That's not a good idea."

"I think it is."

His hand at the small of her back, he ushered
her into the room. Kristie snapped on the light.
She was suddenly aware of the tiny space and the
bed that seemed to take up every inch of space.

Zan pulled her toward him. He gave her another
heart-wrenching kiss. Kristie's conscience warred
with her. Her focus should be on her son and not
on this man she felt so comfortable with. He was
nothing like Earl. Zan was responsible, dependable,
and trustworthy. He was someone you could count
on through thick and thin.

"I think you should go," she said, not really wanting him to go.

"And why is that?" Zan's fingers grazed her cheeks and she couldn't think of a suitable answer.

"Because," Kristie said eventually, "having you here with me is too tempting."

Zan's answer was to pull her down on the bed beside him. "Tempt me."

It had been a long time since she'd made love with a man. She missed that special feeling of being so close that your bodies were one. But making love to Zan would only ruin things between them. She liked the man too much and suspected she might even be in love with him. What if things didn't work out? They were such different people.

"Kristie," Zan said, "make love with me."

He'd already slid one of the straps of her dress down and his lips nibbled her bare shoulder. Kristie's body began a slow burn. She couldn't think, couldn't get the words out to say that this was wrong, she was his client, he her attorney.

"I don't know," Kristie said, giving in to his kisses.

"I do know. I knew from the moment I laid eyes on you that I wanted you. That you were a woman I would never forget."

It was the wine talking. It had to be. Zan McManus's world was far removed from hers. He moved in the circle of beautiful people, and a struggling teacher who was barely able to make ends meet was far from that. He was successful and worldly, a far cry from her.

Still it was nice to have someone to lean on, someone she could trust. Was it so bad to take the comfort he offered even if it were only for one night?

"Come on, hon," Zan said, sliding down the other strap of her dress. He rained kisses in the hollow of her neck and blew against her skin with his sweet breath.

Kristie's arms tightened around his neck. She kissed him back with urgency. He lowered her onto the mattress and kissed her again. She forgot about everything except him. In a fog she realized her dress was being unzipped and pulled over her head. She heard his sharp intake of breath as his hands trailed down her body and he bent over to kiss her skin.

She wanted him naked, wanted to feel every inch of him. She tugged at his shirt and grabbed his belt buckle. He stopped her, slipping off the shirt himself and fumbling with his belt buckle. Zan's sweet musky scent invaded her nostrils. His muscular body pressed against hers.

"Do you have protection?" she thought to ask.

"In my wallet, baby. It will take me just seconds to get it."

Warning lights flashed on. She should have known that someone like Zan would come prepared. He wasn't like her, a person who hadn't had sex in over a year.

Zan got up to retrieve his pants. He went through his pockets and returned with a foil package.

As he settled between her thighs, she stroked his back. His sinewy muscles jumped under her palms. Zan's skin felt like velvet, smooth to the touch. His buttocks were high and firm and his erection pulsated against her sex.

Sheer madness. She should be struck down for even considering making love with her attorney. But overnight Zan had become much more than an attorney, he was her friend. Although no friend that she knew of would be touching her like this, unfolding the soft petals at her core and moving inside to explore. Kristie nibbled on his ear. Her hands stroked Zan's nape. She pressed against him, opened up, and invited him in.

Zan filled her up. He lay still for a moment before he began to thrust. A euphoric feeling came over Kristie, one she had never experienced before. She gasped and cried out his name. Zan drove into her, unleashing his need.

Kristie didn't want him gentle. She wanted to feel every inch of him inside her. She hadn't felt for a long time, not since her son had disappeared, and she'd become numb. But numb was hardly how she felt as the first orgasm ripped through her. She screamed Zan's name.

"I'm here, baby. I'm here."

His warm seed filled the condom he'd used to protect himself. Kristie vaguely registered the ringing phone.

"What awful timing," Zan groaned. He rolled off of her, disposed of the rubber, and searched for his cellular phone.

Horrible timing. But if that ringing phone brought news of her son she was not about to complain.

As wonderful as Zan's loving was, Curtis came first.

Chapter 19

"Hey, did I wake you?" Bill Federicks asked.

Zan tried his best to focus on what the man was saying, though he was still in a fog. Making love to Kristie had been a mind-blowing experience. He hadn't expected that level of passion coming from her, and he hadn't expected to feel the way that he did. He wanted to wrap her in his arms forever.

"What's up?" Zan asked when he trusted himself to speak.

"I'm sorry I'm calling this late. I left a message at the U.S. embassy for someone to get in touch with me, and they just did."

"At this hour?"

Bill chuckled. "This is Mexico. People eat late. My contact probably just got back from dinner. Speaking of which, how was yours?"

"Quite delightful. What do you have?"

Zan heard Kristie stir behind him. He knew she was listening intently to the one-sided conversation.

He turned and placed a finger to his lips. They might be consenting adults but Bill didn't need to know their business.

"I think I got something," Bill said.

"Just tell me."

Kristie was up and off the bed. She placed an arm around his waist and he angled the phone so that they could both hear the conversation.

"A note was delivered to the embassy today. Some woman claims that she's been caring for Curtis these last couple of days."

There was an audible gasp from Kristie.

"What was that?" Bill asked.

"Nothing. Who is this woman? Where does she live?"

"All I got was that she's an American recluse who makes her home in the mountains. She left specific instructions that she would only turn Curtis over to his mother or a person she designated."

"Give me the phone," Kristie hissed.

Zan ignored her. "You've done good work, Bill. Does this woman have a phone number?"

"None that I know of. She left her address and suggested that someone get back to her by way of a note. She wants nothing to do with the police but did offer to bring Curtis into town and leave him at a prearranged spot. She stipulated that his mother or a suitable guardian pick him up."

"Tomorrow, first thing, we're going to the mountains," Zan said. "Come by at seven, we'll leave from here."

Zan hung up and turned to Kristie, who was still clinging to him as if they were bonded.

"Is Curtis okay?" she asked.

"As far as I know. Hopefully tomorrow we'll see for ourselves."

There was an extended silence. Zan realized Kristie was on the brink of tears. As he held her, a vivid memory of the mother he'd been reunited with over twenty-odd years ago surfaced. Things would have been different if she'd come looking for him. He would definitely not be the person he was today.

But one good thing had come from hooking up with his mother again. He'd learned where he'd gotten his middle name. Zan was an abbreviated version of Zanzibar, an island off of the east coast of Africa. Timothy had been his given name. As a tribute to Daphne, he now used the name T. Zan McManus. Timothy had been his mother's legacy to him.

"Zan, is something wrong?" Kristie asked, putting voice to her fears.

He'd almost forgotten about her, and almost forgotten why he was here. A little boy would need him tomorrow, a boy who would have many questions, most requiring diplomacy to answer.

"Nothing's wrong," he said, gathering Kristie close. "Will you be able to sleep?"

"I doubt it," she said. "I can't wait to see Curtis and hold him."

Kristie began crying. Zan held her convulsing body and spoke to her, uttering words of reassurance. How had he ever existed without this vulnerable but gutsy woman in his life? She might not fit into the busy world of an attorney but somehow he would make her fit.

This would be something to ponder upon later. Right now he was taking her back to bed. Sex would be awesome now, without the worry of Curtis hanging over their heads.

Ed walked with Lizette into the dimly lit bar nodding at several engrossed young men playing pool. They were being cheered on by friends swilling beer.

Lizette hadn't even known the place existed until now. It was near the Long Island Railroad Station, close to Sunrise Boulevard. Everyone seemed to know everyone.

"Hey, buddy, haven't see you in a while," a man said, sliding off his stool and approaching Ed. "Who do you got there?"

Ed eased Lizette forward and made introductions. "This here's Lizette Stokes, my lady friend," he said.

Lizette got the distinct impression she was being carefully examined to see if she measured up. Ed had elevated her to the position of girlfriend and she wasn't sure how she felt about that. They had no understanding but it made her feel good that he'd taken the time to introduce her.

Lizette shook the man's hand as he introduced himself.

"I'm Sam, a friend of this deadbeat," the silver-haired man said.

"Nice to meet you, Sam."

They continued on, finding a seat at a booth in the back. "How do you know Sam?" Lizette asked once they were seated.

"He's a retired cop. We used to work at the same precinct. We get together every once in a while to play pool."

"That's nice you keep in touch. You look exhausted."

"It's been a helluva day," Ed admitted. "Right before I left, a call came in from the Mexican authorities. They think they've found Curtis."

Lizette was instantly alert and focused. "Think?"

Ed explained that a note had been sent to the U.S. embassy and that it sounded like an American woman had been caring for Curtis.

"So what's the next step?" Lizette asked.

"The Mexican police are going to contact this lady. If she does have Curtis, then they'll arrange to have him sent back to the United States."

"Did you tell them his mother was on the island? Do they know how to get in touch with Kristie?"

"We told them what we knew," Ed said, signaling the waitress over and quickly switching the conversation. "Get me a beer and a glass of Kendall Jackson for the lady. I'd also like the Buffalo wings. Make them spicy and hot."

After the waitress left, Ed continued. "Some private eye's been nosing around Isle de Artistes. I think your friend retained him. The guy contacted the embassy and some dumb employee told him about the note."

"Good. That means Kristie knows about Curtis."

Ed grunted. "Yeah, I suppose. Just what we need, amateur involvement."

Lizette was glad to see the waitress appear. It saved her from saying something she would later regret. The woman set down tangy chicken designed to clear the sinuses, then placed Ed's beer and Lizette's wine on the table.

Lizette took a deep breath before starting in. "I

don't give a damn about who finds Curtis, just as long as he's been found. I couldn't care less about your politics. All I know is that my girlfriend has been through a rough time. Having your child abducted by a drug addict father who gets arrested is stressful enough."

Ed had the grace to look sheepish. "I see your point," he admitted, giving her puppy dog eyes. "Want to drop the subject and talk about us?"

"Is there an us?" Lizette snapped.

"Come on, honey, we're good together."

They were good in bed but in other ways they were incompatible. Ed was judgmental and a linear thinker, while Lizette saw and accepted the world with all its peaks and valleys. Still, he'd brought out a side of her that she hadn't known existed. She'd become uninhibited and sexy. Ed Sloan, player or not, was fun.

Ed had devoured three-quarters of the chicken by the time Lizette tasted her first piece. He was also working on his third beer. Lizette sipped on her wine, agonizing over how this would end. *Don't make the mistake of falling in love with him,* the logical part of her brain screamed.

"You about done?" Ed asked, as Lizette dabbed at her lips and crumpled the paper napkin in her fist.

"Yes, I'm full."

Ed crooked a finger at the waitress and called for the check. He slapped down some bills and stood.

"What say we go back to your place and work off these calories?" His hand slapped her buttocks as she stood. "Love your rump, it's even nicer than J. Lo's."

Liar. But it was nice to know that Ed liked her big butt and made sure everyone knew it.

Curtis could see his mother clear as day as he got off the small airplane that had taken him back to America. Kristie, his mom, was waiting with arms outstretched. Curtis began running toward her. As he got close he realized it wasn't his mother waiting after all. His father had appeared from somewhere and he had two policemen with him just like he'd had in the newspaper picture. Curtis started backing off as the men clamped handcuffs on his dad and began dragging him away. He opened his mouth and screamed.

Strong arms held him tight and a soft bosom provided a pillow for his head. A female voice said, "Honey, wake up. It's only a dream."

Curtis opened his eyes. Moonbeam had set a candle down on the dresser and her anxious expression told him she was concerned. "What was the dream about?" she asked.

Curtis, realizing that he was safe, told her.

"Maybe it means that your mother is close by. Maybe she came to get you," Moonbeam said. "Jose should have delivered the note by now."

Curtis hoped so.

"I'm going to lie down next to you until you fall asleep," Moonbeam said.

"Promise?" Curtis begged, knowing he must sound like a baby. But even now, strange shadows danced across the ceiling, and the darkness hid monsters in the corners.

"I promise. Now you go to sleep."

Moonbeam's body was warm and she smelled like the vegetables she grew in her back garden. Curtis squeezed his eyes tight and imagined he was home in his own bed. Outside he heard chirping noises that Moonbeam explained were crickets. The goats were putting up a fuss and the wind rattled the windows.

He was suddenly very tired. His eyelids drooped. Maybe he would go to sleep and maybe when he woke up something good would happen. Maybe his mother would be there and she would tell him that this was just an adventure.

He liked adventures. But only if they were fun.

Chapter 20

"Bill, you've done a bang-up job," Zan said. "You were able to find out where this Moonbeam person lives."

Bill rolled his eyes. "Trust me, it wasn't easy. The woman's a strange duck, a throwback from the hippie era. She's dropped out of life. She's been living on Isle de Artistes for over ten years in this cabin on top of a mountain with no water or electricity."

"Sounds eccentric to me. You've taken a look at your map and figured out the roads?" Zan asked.

"Yup." Bill spread the map on the coffee table and with his index finger traced their route. They were in the lobby of the Villa Rosa and at that early hour there were few people about.

"Can we go?" Kristie asked, heading for the exit. She'd had little sleep. She and Zan had made love until the wee hours of the morning. Now she was wired and operating on caffeine and adrenaline.

They climbed into the Jeep. Kristie sat up front sipping on coffee from a paper cup, while Bill reclined in the back. Soon the little village was left behind and they entered a rural part of the island, heading in the opposite direction from the jail they'd visited yesterday.

It probably would take a good hour for them to get to their destination given the terrain, Kristie figured. Her knees bounced as the men conversed, devising a plan. She'd brought with her a change of clothes for Curtis and his favorite stuffed toy: a dog that was loved so much it had lost an eye.

"Can you imagine an American living like this?" Zan said, pointing out the hovels that sat back from the main thoroughfare.

"It's not the typical American who's made their home here," Bill said. "These are artists. Money and material things mean nothing to them. It's not about prestige or keeping up with the Joneses. It's about being true to themselves."

"Yes, I suppose," Zan said contemplatively. "But you'd have to be a risk taker to give everything up."

"How much longer?" Kristie asked, breaking into their conversation.

"Another twenty minutes or so," Zan said.

"I wonder if Curtis will be happy to see me."

"Why won't he be? He probably misses his mother."

"What if Earl filled his head up with nonsense and he thinks that I've abandoned him?"

"We'll cross that bridge if we come to it," Zan said, his hand stroking her bare knee where her walking shorts ended. "You're giving in to insecurity. Curtis will be ecstatic to see you."

"God, I hope so."

They rode the rest of the way in silence. The road had become increasingly mountainous and the Jeep moaned and groaned as they started up a new incline. They passed several shacks, many of which didn't even have full walls.

Kristie hoped that her son wasn't living in conditions like these. She hoped he had a roof over his head and a soft bed to sleep in. She hoped that Earl hadn't done irreparable damage to his psyche, and that they would not have to deal with months of therapy ahead.

"Turn down that path," Bill ordered, referring to his map.

Zan followed a dirt trail devoid of houses or living beings. Kristie felt a tension headache beginning to build.

"We should be there shortly," Bill said, pointing out a corrugated roof emerging from behind the trees.

Kristie took several deep breaths. She should be grateful to Moonbeam for taking in her son, not critical of the woman's choice of homestead. She should be joyful that Curtis was alive.

"We're here," Bill announced.

Zan stopped in front of a run-down shack that needed a coat of paint. "Looks like someone's beaten us to it."

A black and white car with a siren on the roof was parked directly in front of them. Without thinking, Kristie hopped out of the Jeep and raced toward the shack's front door. Her footsteps faltered as she read the words emblazoned across the other vehicle's door. *Policia*.

Cops?

"Might as well go in and find out what's going on," Zan said, holding on to Kristie's elbow and steering her toward the house. Bill followed closely behind them.

Zan rapped on the front door. Kristie's heart did somersaults and ended up in her throat. Waiting was agony. Footsteps eventually headed their way.

"Yes?" a woman with bushy salt-and-pepper hair inquired. She wore a tie-dyed muumuu.

"I'm Kristie Phillips, Curtis's mother. I'm here to take him home."

"Come in. I see where Curtis gets his looks. I'm Moonbeam. Who are the men with you?"

"I'm Zan McManus, Ms. Phillips's attorney," Zan said. "This is Bill Federicks, a private eye we retained to find Curtis."

"I don't like lawyers or PI's," Moonbeam said, wrinkling her nose. "But I could use an attorney right about now. Why don't you come on in?" She stepped aside.

Two men dressed in navy blue eyed them warily.

"I'm being interrogated by the police," Moonbeam explained.

"Where is my son?" Kristie demanded, not giving a damn about the police.

The two policemen continued a conversation in Spanish as if she did not exist.

"Where is Curtis?" Kristie repeated.

"He was taken into town by the FBI. The police threatened to arrest me."

"What happened to only releasing him to his mother or a designee?" Bill reminded Moonbeam.

"You ever have a gun pointed at your head?"

"Can't say I have," Bill said, softly.

"What were the charges?" Zan challenged, getting into attorney mode.

"Ask them." Moonbeam flipped a thumb in the police's direction. "Things operate a bit differently here than they do in the United States."

"I'm an *abogado*, a lawyer," Zan explained to the men in blue. "What did this woman do wrong?"

One of the policemen found his English. "The senorita would not let us come in. She said we needed a search warrant to enter. She pulled out a shotgun and aimed it at us. We had to knock it out of her hands."

Good for Moonbeam, Kristie thought. She'd put up a good fight before turning Curtis over.

"Where can I find my son?" Kristie demanded of the English-speaking policeman.

"At the police station unless the FBI has taken him to the U.S. embassy."

"We're leaving now," Kristie said to Zan. Remembering her manners, she turned back to Moonbeam. "Thank you for taking such good care of my son. I'll have to think of some way to repay you."

"You already have," Moonbeam answered. "It is karma that made us meet. Positive energy begets positive things."

Kristie whispered to Zan, "We can't just leave and throw her to the wolves. Do something."

Zan reached into his wallet and removed a stack of bills. He handed them to Bill, who laid them on the rickety kitchen table and said to the cops, "Consider this a donation to the Police Officers Benevolent Association. This woman was probably scared to death when she pointed a shotgun at you. I bet you it wasn't even loaded."

Moonbeam gave him a look but did not comment.

The policemen again conversed. One of them pocketed the bills and grunted at them. *"Gracias. This will make our jefe happy."*

"Chief," Zan explained.

Kristie doubted the chief would even see the bribe the two had just accepted. She tugged on Zan's hand. "Now that that's settled, can we go?"

"Absolutely."

"I'm coming with you," Moonbeam said as they headed out. "I'm not remaining behind with these two. It will be good for Curtis to see that you and I met."

Kristie darted a look at Zan. She didn't want a huge group around when she was reunited with her son. But Zan didn't seem fazed and Kristie wondered if there was a master plan.

"Is your business about done now?" Zan asked the cops. "If so, the lady would like to lock up."

"Sí, senor," the police said, ambling out.

When their patrol car drove off, all four got into the Jeep and headed down the mountain.

"Why would anyone take a little boy to the police station?" Kristie asked out loud when they were halfway there.

"Curtis is international news," Zan said dryly. "He's been missing and his father's been arrested and thrown into a Mexican jail. Now he turns up in the mountains cared for by a stranger. The media are probably champing at the bit. The precinct would be the safest place for Curtis to be."

"I'm the only person taking Curtis home," Kristie said firmly.

Zan's hand patted her knee.

She sat back and watched the scenery whiz by, her mind fully focused on her son. It had been almost two weeks since she'd last seen him. Two weeks, an eternity.

Moonbeam hummed softly in the backseat next to Bill. She was a peculiar woman but her heart was in the right place. Kristie did not doubt that Curtis had been well taken care of by his surrogate mother.

Bill consulted his map and periodically gave Zan instructions. They entered the town now awake with enterprising vendors. Zan steered the vehicle down a side street and parked in front of a long, low building. Kristie was out the Jeep like a shot and racing toward the double doors. Zan overtook her.

"Let me handle this," he said.

His hand at the base of her spine, they entered. Bill and Moonbeam trailed them.

A bleary-eyed officer looked up disinterestedly from behind a battered desk.

"*Buenos dias,*" Zan said.

"Good morning."

Zan slapped his business card on the desk and the policeman picked it up and examined it. He remained expressionless. "*Sí?*" he said.

"We're here to collect Curtis Leone," Kristie said, speaking up.

"*Uno momento.*"

With that he was gone. One moment turned into several minutes. Finally he returned with a woman dressed in civilian garb. Kristie guessed that she must be a police officer.

"I'm Kristie Phillips, Curtis's mother," Kristie said, producing her driver's license, which the woman took.

"And I'm Ms. Phillips's lawyer, T. Zan McManus," Zan said. "The people with us are friends."

"Ms. Phillips, I'm so glad you're here," the tiny Caucasian woman who looked more like a teenager said. "I'm Special Agent Linda Parsons. I'm glad you took the trip, your son's been through a lot."

"Where's Curtis?" Kristie demanded. "Where's my son?"

"In a back room. I gave him a teddy bear. Holding a stuffed toy often helps when a child has been traumatized."

Kristie remembered the dog that she'd brought along for Curtis. "I want to see him now." She advanced on the little woman.

"We'd both like to see him," Zan said.

Zan had been wonderful but this meeting needed to take place between mother and son. "I'd like to see Curtis alone."

There was a pained expression on Zan's face as he turned away. Kristie realized she'd hurt his feelings. She'd make it up to him later. She needed this time with Curtis. She needed to talk to him, touch him, and reestablish the special bond they'd had. It would be difficult with a stranger looking over her shoulder. And Zan was a stranger to Curtis.

"As you wish," Zan said, his professional tone firmly in place. He stepped back, joining Bill and Moonbeam and giving her space.

Kristie felt awful but her son had to be her priority.

"Come with me," Linda Parsons said, quietly.

Kristie glanced over her shoulder. Zan flipped

her the thumbs-up sign and Bill grinned like the proverbial Cheshire Cat. Moonbeam pumped her arms in the air. The support felt wonderful. Kristie offered them a watery smile.

As she followed the agent down a gloomy corridor Kristie's trepidation built. Agent Parsons was about to turn the knob of a door at the very end when she stopped. "Would you like a few minutes to pull yourself together?"

"No, I'm okay." But she wasn't okay. She had to put aside her murderous feelings about Earl and greet Curtis with all the love and warmth she could summon. She couldn't let her anxiety show.

Kristie entered a room where several policemen stood chatting. A man dressed in a business suit was barking into a cell phone. She scanned the room looking for Curtis and found him seated in a corner clutching a stuffed bear. Her little boy looked tired and dirty but he had his brave face on. His golden skin had darkened from too much time in the sun and his brown curls were streaked with blond. Kristie gulped the tears back.

She forgot about everyone except Curtis. Ignoring introductions, Kristie advanced toward her son. Curtis had still not seen her. He glanced warily around the room. Their eyes connected and held. Curtis was up like a shot, sending the chair he'd been seated on toppling.

"Mommy, Mommy, I thought you didn't want me," he cried, clutching her around the middle and burying his head in her stomach. The teddy bear fell to the floor, forgotten.

Kristie squeezed Curtis's body close. Tears flowed. So much for being calm and collected.

"Honey," she said when she could speak, "you know better than that. Didn't I tell you often enough that I love you more than anything else in the whole world?"

Curtis's light eyes swept her face. "Mommy, why are you crying?"

"Because I'm happy to see you, baby. So very happy."

Curtis clung to her, and she held him tight, glad to have his warm body next to hers, glad that the limb that had been severed was reattached. The awful nightmare that she'd been through was almost forgotten now that she had her child back.

"Where is Daddy?" Curtis asked, lifting his head from her stomach and biting on his lower lip.

The last thing Kristie wanted to do was talk about Earl, but Curtis deserved an answer.

"Your dad's being held in a special place. Maybe he'll get some help at last."

"I heard Moonbeam say that he had done something bad. I saw the newspaper," Curtis said, his lips trembling.

Kristie thought quickly. Avoidance was the only answer. "It wasn't nice of your father to take you away and not tell me where he'd taken you to. I was worried and scared."

"Me too."

Kristie kissed her child.

"When can we go home, Mom?" Curtis asked.

"Soon," Kristie promised.

"Ms. Phillips?" The guy in the suit interrupted, placing a hand on Kristie's shoulder. "We'd like you to sit and answer some questions. We'll need to make arrangements to get you and Curtis home."

Kristie remembered Zan waiting outside. "My attorney needs to be here if you're going to grill me."

The agent seemed genuinely puzzled. Kristie couldn't decide whether he was faking it or not. "Why would you need an attorney, ma'am?"

"Because I want one. Mr. McManus accompanied me here, and anything you have to ask can be discussed in his presence."

Linda Parsons, who seemed a pleasant enough sort, took over. "Our questions are mere formalities."

"Get me Zan," Kristie said, sticking to her guns.

"Who's Zan?" Curtis asked, his bottom lip trembling again.

"A friend."

Kristie sat in the chair the male FBI agent held out and settled Curtis on her lap. The stranglehold he placed on her neck left her short of breath.

After a lengthy, silent exchange Linda Parsons left to find Zan.

Kristie sat quietly holding Curtis and waiting for Zan to come. She needed his commanding presence but she did not need him to take care of her.

She sensed his arrival before she even saw him. The agents had grown quiet and the room seemed to have shrunk. Although he was casually dressed in a polo shirt and Dockers, Zan's presence brought with it respect.

"Is there a reason Ms. Phillips is being held?" he demanded. Zan smiled at Curtis and he smiled his toothless smile back.

"She's not being held. We're just talking," the agent in the business suit said.

"My client will not be responding to questions. Her son was taken overseas without her permission and she's had a difficult time of it. Kristie, are you about ready to leave?"

"This matter is being handled by the Federal Bureau of Investigation," Navy Suit barked, pulling himself up to his full six feet.

Zan stared at him, one imperious brow half cocked. "Is Ms. Phillips a suspect?"

The agent hesitated. "No, I can't say she is. At least not now."

"I thought not," Zan said. "Kristie, hon, you're free to leave. Let's get Curtis home."

Curtis looked at his mother and then at Zan. "Is he coming with us?"

"Yes, he is. We're going home, sweetie," Kristie said, holding out a hand to her son and offering the other to Zan.

Zan flipped his business card in the FBI's direction. "If there are further questions I'll be glad to answer them. You may reach me at my business address on Monday."

Zan took Kristie's hand. Flanked by her two favorite guys she walked out. She'd never felt so cherished or so loved.

Chapter 21

The prisoners were allowed out in the yard for recreation once a day, most of which consisted of walking up and down, and bumming cigarettes or other coveted objects from those willing to trade. Earl and the prison guard, Jesus, were off to the side conducting their daily transaction. Almost all of Earl's money that he'd gotten from selling his watch was used up. The only thing he had left to sell was his ring, a ring that Kristie had given him when they got married, and that he once loved. But it was only a material thing.

"Has my ex-wife or the Tom she's been screwing posted my bail?" Earl asked the prison guard who'd just slipped him a joint in exchange for money.

"Tom as in Tomas? What does that mean?"

Dumb ass.

"Never mind," Earl replied, pocketing the blunt. "If you're not African-American you probably

wouldn't know. Just find out if money's been paid
to get me the hell out of here."

Jesus nodded. But Earl wasn't sure he understood what he was really asking.

A couple of days back, Earl had sold his wrist-
watch for pitifully few American dollars. He'd needed something to ease the agony when the shakes
took over, and Jesus had come through. It hadn't
taken Earl long to figure out that bribery and cor-
ruption reigned in a Mexican jail. Privileges were
granted to those that could afford them, and the
U.S. dollar bought some unique perks.

Jesus had immediately shifted his allegiance from
a male prostitute when Earl had offered his Nikes
up. It had taken Earl a while to get used to being
barefooted but the constant supply of grass that Jesus
now kept him in made stepping over feces and
other bodily wastes worthwhile. Drugs had made
existing in this hellhole so much easier.

Earl would have to think of something soon if
he ended up staying any longer in this dismal place.
Other than the ring, there was nothing left to sell
except for his body and even he didn't sink that
low.

"You'll have to get me more *dinero* soon if you
want other stuff," Jesus said, echoing his thoughts.

Earl nodded contemplatively. "Okay. But first
you find out about my bail."

Jesus nodded and strutted off. Earl eyed the other
prisoners warily. He had not made many friends
amongst them primarily because he did not speak
Spanish. He was also the only black man incarcer-
ated, and he was regarded with fascination and a
great deal of suspicion. In many ways that was good.

He wasn't subjected to the bullying that took place right in front of the prison guards' faces, and which they turned a blind eye to. The others were scared of him.

The world around Earl ebbed and receded as the herb took full effect. He barely registered a young man advancing, and when he did he suspected that he was there to grub a cigarette.

"*Hola*, amigo," the young man said.

Earl knew enough to figure out he was being greeted and waited to see what was coming next.

The man pointed to his left hand and said, "*Bonita.*"

There was no mistaking what he was up to. He wanted Earl's ring, a ring he wasn't prepared to give up.

Earl ignored him and began to walk away. The man tugged on the back of Earl's shirt, forcing him to turn back.

"The ring."

Even if Earl had wanted to hand it over, the humidity had swollen his knuckles and it would be painful taking the thing off.

"What ring?" Earl asked, playing dumb.

"That one. It is *oro* and worth something, no?"

"It's my wedding band."

Earl saw a glint of metal as it flashed in front of his face. He realized the young man meant business and tried to yank the ring off. It wouldn't budge.

The sharp metal blade was pressed to his side and he lost control of his bladder as he stared into the man's red eyes. Urine trickled down Earl's leg and there were laughter and taunts from behind as the other prisoners witnessed what was going on.

The more Earl pulled on his finger the more the ring refused to yield.

"You need help?" his accoster asked, jabbing the knife into Earl's side.

Earl dared to look down at the crimson ring that was beginning to soak his shirt and at the blood that dripped onto the parched ground. Feeling faint, he looked to heaven but even it had begun to blur. He could no longer hear the prisoners' taunts and could no longer feel the hot sun. His knees buckled and there was a ringing in his ears. He attempted to grasp for something that would keep him upright but there wasn't anything concrete nearby. He fell with a thud onto the hard ground and blackness enveloped him.

"Paging Senora Kristie Phillips. Mrs. Phillips, please return to the Mexicana desk for a phone call," the announcement said.

"Mom, isn't that you?" Curtis said, tugging on Kristie's arm.

"I wonder what that's about," Zan said, casting a puzzled look her way.

"Your guess is as good as mine. I'm tempted to ignore that page. I just want to get on the plane and go home."

The phone call couldn't have come at a worse time, minutes before Kristie, Zan, and Curtis were supposed to board their plane to the United States. Bill had left on an earlier flight, and Moonbeam, who had insisted on coming to the airport, had wished them all the karma in the world. She'd waved them through security with tears in her eyes.

"We're now boarding first-class passengers and those needing special assistance," the agent from behind the Mexicana desk announced.

A handful of people trickled toward the boarding gate.

The announcement came again. "Paging Mrs. Phillips. Mrs. Phillips, please pick up the closest Mexicana courtesy phone."

"Mom," Curtis whined, "aren't you going to answer that?"

Kristie's stomach told her it wasn't good news. Zan's expression had also turned grim.

"Why don't we find out if there's a courtesy phone nearby so that you don't have to go through security again?" he said, turning and heading off to speak with the Mexicana boarding agent.

Kristie held Curtis's hand and trailed him.

Another announcement followed. "We're boarding passengers from the rear. Those holding seats numbers thirty through twenty-three may now proceed on board."

Kristie's anxiety began to build. She wanted to get on board that plane. Lovely as Isle de Artistes was, she'd had enough of Mexico. She needed to get her son home.

Zan was speaking in rapid Spanish to the agent, and Kristie only caught a couple of words. Words like *policia . . . importante . . . su esposo.* It was enough to make her want to turn around and run down the jetway. Zan, sensing she was behind him, turned around.

"What is it?" Kristie asked, careful to keep her voice neutral.

"I don't know. The phone call is from the police. They're insisting they speak to you."

Kristie knew with certainty then that something was wrong. "Do we have time for me to take this call?" she asked the gate agent.

"*Sí.* If you make it quick."

Kristie grabbed the phone the agent held out, ignoring Zan's restraining hand on her back.

He whispered, "You've got your son. We should hightail it out of here."

"This is Kristie Phillips," Kristie said.

A guttural voice barked, "Senora Phillips. *Su esposo* is in the hospital. He's been stabbed."

Kristie's head whirled. She couldn't hold back the words that rushed out. "How could that happen?" She didn't bother explaining that she was not a senora but a senorita, and no longer had a husband. Curtis's anxious little face looked up at her.

She pulled herself together and made her voice sound normal. "Mr. Leone has family in Arizona. Maybe you should call them. He'll be needing their support."

There was a harrumphing on the other end as the policeman cleared his throat. "He's asking for his wife, ma'am."

"I'm no longer Earl's wife. What exactly is his condition?"

"He's stable now that the bleeding has stopped."

Kristie whooshed out a breath. Earl wasn't dying. Zan's voice came from behind her.

"We've got to go."

Kristie covered the mouthpiece of the phone and whispered, "I feel awful. Earl's been hurt."

"He's no longer your problem. You can call his family when you get to the United States."

"I could do that," she said, contemplating.

"Mrs. Phillips?" the policeman on the other end said.

"Ms. Phillips. I'm about to get on a plane. Someone from Earl's family will be in touch." She hung up.

It was one of the most difficult things Kristie had ever done. But she had to sever the ties from Earl. He was way beyond her help and she wasn't responsible for him. She would make the call to his family and then the rest was in their hands. Whether they chose to leave him languishing in jail would be up to them. It was time for Kristie Phillips to move on.

She took the hand Zan offered and together with Curtis boarded the plane.

"Mom, will Dad be okay?" Curtis asked when they were seated.

"I hope so, son." Kristie ran her fingers through her son's tight curls and said, "Say your prayers and wish your dad well."

Zan leaned over them and said, "It was a brave thing you did, Kristie Phillips. I'm proud of you." He turned to Curtis. "I love your mother, son. Do you think you can make room in your life for one other person?"

Curtis stared at Zan for a long time before solemnly nodding his head.

It was the first time that Zan had said he loved her and his words were sweeter than wine. Kristie looked at Zan over Curtis's head, then looked away. His eyes communicated his love. The plane's engines started up and they taxied down the runway. Kristie thought about how different they were and wondered if love would be enough. She'd failed miserably in her marriage, and starting up another relationship was scary.

"I love you," Zan repeated as the plane rose into the air.

She did too. Zan McManus was like no other man she'd met before.

"That scumbag Earl Leone has managed to get himself stabbed," Ed said to officer John Banks after hanging up the phone.

"Figures he would come to a bad end," John answered, lazily, keeping his feet propped up on the desk. He chewed on a toothpick and stared at the far wall.

The call had just come in from Mexico. The authorities were nervous that an American citizen locked up in their jail had been stabbed by an inmate. They wanted Earl Leone the hell out of there. Earl was screaming for legal representation and his family was threatening to get the American media involved.

"Didn't you say the guy has family in Arizona?" John said to Ed.

"Yeah, but I don't think they're on speaking terms."

"That might be so, but the ex obviously wants nothing to do with the guy. She's ticked off that he ran away with her son, then got himself in a jam."

"And she has every right to be."

"Since when are you on her side?" John asked,

sliding the toothpick out of his mouth and regarding Ed suspiciously.

"Since we're hard pressed to prove that this was a scam. Lizette's known Kristie Phillips since she started teaching school. She said she's a good sort and very devoted to her kid."

"You've done a quick turnaround," John said, eyeing Ed. "Sounds like this Lizette's gotten to you."

"She has. I was wrong about Kristie Phillips. I couldn't understand why she was dragging her feet, and why it took her forever to go public with news of her son's abduction. I think she was scared and maybe a little timid to let other people in her life."

"Sounds like Lizette's done a good job of convincing you that the Phillips woman's a good egg."

"Keep Lizette out of this," Ed said, getting to his feet and glancing at the clock. His shift was almost over and he planned on stopping by to see Lizette.

"Hey, what happened to the guy who liked overtime?" John asked as Ed grabbed his jacket.

"That guy has a life now," Ed said, slipping the jacket on but not zipping it. "I'm off tomorrow. Think you can manage?"

John narrowed his eyes but didn't answer him, and Ed headed out.

Twenty minutes later he'd parked his SUV in front of Lizette's apartment. As had become his custom he hadn't bothered to call. Ed was counting on her being home.

He wasn't disappointed when he pressed on her bell and he heard a rustling inside as she approached the keyhole.

"Who is it?" Lizette asked as if she didn't know.

"Open up, babe."

"Oh, it's you," she said, throwing the door wide.

Ed stepped inside, a grin spreading slowly over his face. From the way she was dressed he could tell she'd been expecting him. The grin quickly changed to a leer as he took in the slinky red nightgown that hugged every curve and told him clearly that she wore nothing underneath it.

"You getting ready for bed?" he growled.

"Do I look like it?" Lizette said, teasing him. "Want a beer?"

"You know it, hon."

He had a proposition for her, one he hoped she would like.

"How much are you paying for this place?" he asked when Lizette had set a cold can of Bud in front of him.

"Why are you asking?"

"Just asking."

"You're a police officer. You don't just make idle conversation."

Lizette stood in front of him, hands on her hips. The silky material of the gown bunched, and his eyes rose to her ample breasts. God, what was he doing drinking beer when he could have one of those nipples in his mouth?

Ed set down the can and patted his lap for Lizette to sit. She eased gingerly down and wrapped her hands around his neck. "Talk to me."

"It's like this," Ed said. "I was thinking we should move in together. Share expenses and such."

"We should do what?"

At first Ed thought he was about to be rebuffed but one look at her expression told him that she was in shock. He pressed his advantage.

"We're good together, babe, and it's not like we're in our twenties. I'm talking commitment here. If this living together thing works out, then we'll discuss getting married."

There was a long stretch of silence and he held his breath. For the first time in his life he felt nervous. Most of the women he'd been involved with were always nagging at him to settle down with them. Their constant whining had made him run.

"You think we can make it together?" Lizette asked, her heart in her eyes.

"I'm willing to give it a try. What about you?"

"Whose place would we move into?" she asked.

Ed shrugged. "I have no particular attachment to mine, but it is bigger."

"Yes, but mine's rent-controlled."

"Settled then," Ed said, kissing her and claiming the breasts that had taunted him from the minute he arrived.

They came up for air several minutes later. "I can't wait to tell Kristie we're moving in together," Lizette said.

Ed stood up and handed her his cell phone.

Chapter 22

"We have a story with a happy ending," Ryan Velox announced. "Kristie Phillips and her son were reunited two days ago on a small Mexican island where American expatriates live. Ms. Phillips denied our request for a live interview but she did speak with us from the comfort of her home and had this to say."

The camera panned to Kristie.

"Mom, that's you," Curtis said excitedly. "And there I am."

She, Zan, and Curtis were seated in Kristie's living room. Kristie had invited him to dinner and then to watch her interview. Curtis needed the stability of being in his own home right now and although Zan had offered to take them out to dinner, she'd turned him down.

It still amazed her how well Curtis and Zan got along. Zan had not pushed himself on the child but had allowed Curtis to find his own way. They'd

eaten their dinner of pizza together and now they
sat on the couch watching television.

Kristie had made the call to Earl's family as promised and predictably they'd been cold. But she'd
said what she needed to say and now the rest was up
to them. The family wasn't rich but could certainly
afford to retain an attorney to help their son. Zan
had recommended a colleague that wasn't too expensive and Kristie had passed that information on.

Ryan Velox droned on. "This is one happy ending to what has not been a happy situation. This is
Ryan Velox signing off."

"He's done a good job and deserves his promotion," Kristie said, snapping the television off.

It had just been announced that Ryan Velox was
moving into the prime-time anchor spot.

"Time to go to bed, young man," Zan said, bend-
ing over and gesturing to Curtis to get on his back.

With a squeal of laughter, Curtis happily com-
plied. Kristie considered this bonding time, so she
remained where she was. She kissed her son and
sent him off knowing that he was in good hands.
Curtis knew the routine: find his pajamas in his
bottom drawer, wash his face and brush his teeth,
then say his prayers and get into bed. Zan had
promised to read him a story and before it ended,
Curtis would be asleep. After that she and Zan
would have time together.

A half hour later, Zan shut off Curtis's lights.
Her son was fast asleep clutching the stuffed dog
that had only one eye. Kristie picked up the mess
that Curtis had made in the living room.

"He's asleep at last," she said, stacking a bunch
of comic books one on top of the other.

"Out like a light. How are you holding up?"

"I'm beat," she admitted.

Kristie had returned to school the day after they arrived from Mexico, stating that she did not want to take advantage since it had been nice of the principal to give her this time.

Emotionally she was still drained. It had been an exhausting several weeks with Curtis missing and Earl getting into trouble. But as Ryan Velox said it had worked out well.

Zan knew it was now or never. As every day went by, it became increasingly clearer that he couldn't just let Kristie go. Despite his reservations about having a ready-made family, he and Curtis had bonded and could be mistaken for father and son. He was attached to the boy and loved his mother. So what was there to debate? It was time for him to make them a family.

He knew others might argue that he had known Kristie for a relatively short time, but in fact it seemed like an eternity to him. They'd gone through so much together.

Curtis, with the help of a therapist, had bounded back quickly. He seemed to be taking it in stride that there was a good possibility he might not see his father for quite a long time, and then only if visits were supervised.

Zan had pushed Kristie to go back to court. He was quite certain that a judge hearing her story would rule in her favor and renege on Earl's visitation rights. Earl was a criminal. Given the circumstances of his arrest he would be declared an unfit

father. But Kristie, compassionate soul that she
was, didn't want to cut Earl entirely out of Curtis's
life. She and Zan were still in negotiation on this
point.

Zan now admitted that the weakness he'd seen
in Kristie, which so reminded him of his mother,
was in actuality not a weakness at all but a deep de-
sire to avoid conflict or draw attention to herself.
She'd proven herself strong when she needed to
be. And the fact that she still insisted on paying
her legal bill proved to him that she wasn't going
to be totally dependent on him.

He wouldn't have a clinging, weeping woman
on his hands when he came home late. He wouldn't
have one that was constantly calling him to come
home. What he would have was a gorgeous help-
mate who would insist on working and contribut-
ing to their life. He liked the entire package, liked
that he wouldn't be pressed to produce an heir right
off. In a couple of years, they could discuss expand-
ing their family when the law practice his grandfather had built would be on more solid ground.

"What are you thinking about?" Kristie asked.

"Us."

She looked at him with those tawny eyes of hers.
"Okay, give it to me. You want out."

"On the contrary," he said, gathering her close.
"I want us to get married and have a future together."

Kristie went dead still in his arms. "You want to
get married?"

"Yes, I do."

"You want to marry me? Why?"

"Because I love you and I adore your son."

"But we've been nothing but problems."

"No, you've been nothing but answers to the dilemma I've been in," he said, kissing her.

"What am I going to do about my house?"

"Is that a yes?" Zan asked, kissing her again. He knew he was sure. No one tasted like Kristie in the whole wide world.

"I guess," Kristie said when she came up for breath.

"That's a lukewarm response and highly unacceptable."

"It's a yes," she said, her eyes twinkling.

"Then your house can be sold and the proceeds used to pay me the money you owe me," he said, winking at her.

"Spoken like the attorney you are. And it will certainly save me the trouble and aggravation of taking out a loan."

"Now you're talking."

Zan pulled Kristie down on the couch to sit next to him. He began kissing her with ardor and she kissed him back. His hands were all over her and she pressed into him, wanting and apparently needing more.

Zan's hands were on her breasts when he remembered their sleeping child. "We should take this into the bedroom and lock the door," he suggested.

"Yes, let's. And by the way, Timothy, I do love you."

"Timothy, where did that come from?" Zan pretended to glare at her.

Kristie refused to break the stare. She wasn't the least bit intimidated by him. "You mentioned that name the first time I met you and I sneaked a look at your passport, verifying that it was true."

"No one calls me Timothy," Zan growled.

"I will," she said, holding his hand and walking with him to her bedroom. She waited until he'd locked the door before saying, "But I do like Zan better. Tonight I intend to show my strong African prince just how much I do."

"I'm waiting for you to put your money where your mouth is," Zan said, slipping off his clothes and getting under the covers.

Kristie did a slow striptease and stood in front of him butt-naked. "You're forgetting something," she said.

Zan scratched his head and looked at her.

She prompted him. "I . . ."

"I love you," he said, springing from the bed and picking her up. "With my heart, and with my soul, and I have every intention of showing you how much. Now come here, woman."

And Kristie did, showing him that she was his.

God had been very good to them. Kristie loved Zan with her heart and soul. In time, they would expand their little family. It felt good to come home.

Dear Reader:

Did you know that as of March 31, 2003 there were 97,297 missing persons cases in the United States alone? And 54,184 of these cases were juveniles.

My heart breaks every time I hear about one of these children. I can only imagine what it must be like to sit by a phone, hoping that your child, or someone who has seen him, is on the other end. Often these children have been abducted by a parent or someone they know.

Hopefully none of my readers have lived through this heartbreaking experience. But if such a thing happens, you must be prepared to take action.

Here are some helpful hints:

Immediately call 911. (There is no 24 or 48 hour waiting period.)

Notify the Federal Bureau of Investigation.

Log onto *www.beyondmissing.com*. this is a free service that allows registered law enforcement to create and distribute flyers. Parents can also create and distribute flyers as well.

Notify all local news media.

Notify your local non-profit child locator service.

Contact the National Center For Missing and Exploited Children at 1 800-The-Lost

Make sure your home phone is always attended by someone your child knows.

Try to maintain your physical and emotional well-being.

And finally, never give up hope.

Would love to hear from you,

Marcia King-Gamble
www.lovemarcia.com
Mkinggambl@aol.com
P.O. Box 25143
Tamarac, FL 33320

ABOUT THE AUTHOR

Marcia King-Gamble is a Caribbean-American novelist who makes Florida her home. She is the author of ten novels and two novellas. An ex-travel industry executive, Marcia has seen most of the world. She has spent time in the Far East and traveled throughout Europe. Venice and New Zealand are two of her most recent discoveries. It is a coin toss as to which she enjoys most.

Marcia was first published in 1998 and has been nominated for awards by both *Affaire de Coeur* and *Romantic Times* magazines. Her first mainstream, titled, *Jade*, was a finalist for the prestigious Maggie award.

Marcia is currently the director of student services at the Writers and Artists Institute in South Florida.